For Luke ♡ **W9-BNW-136**

With love — mom

2001

LORD OF THE
NUTCRACKER MEN

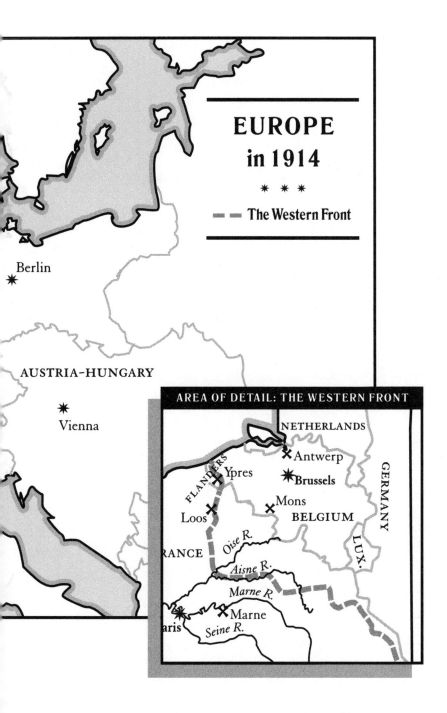

EUROPE in 1914

✳ ✳ ✳

━ ━ The Western Front

Berlin ✳

AUSTRIA–HUNGARY

Vienna ✳

AREA OF DETAIL: THE WESTERN FRONT

NETHERLANDS

✖ Antwerp

FLANDERS

✖ Ypres

✳ Brussels

Loos ✖

✖ Mons

BELGIUM

GERMANY

FRANCE

Oise R.

LUX.

Aisne R.

Marne R.

Paris ✳

✖ Marne

Seine R.

LORD OF THE
NUTCRACKER MEN

❖

IAIN LAWRENCE

DELACORTE PRESS

Published by
Delacorte Press
an imprint of
Random House Children's Books
a division of Random House, Inc.
1540 Broadway
New York, New York 10036

Visit us on the Web! www.randomhouse.com/teens
Educators and librarians, for a variety of teaching tools, visit us at
www.randomhouse.com/teachers

Library of Congress Cataloging-in-Publication Data
Lawrence, Iain
    Lord of the Nutcracker men / Iain Lawrence.
        p.   cm.
    Summary: An English boy during World War I comes to believe that the battles he enacts with his toy soldiers control the war his father is fighting on the front.
    ISBN 0-385-72924-3 (trade) — ISBN 0-385-90024-4 (lib. bdg.)
    1. World War, 1914–1918—England—Juvenile fiction. 2. World War, 1914–1918—France—Juvenile fiction. [1. World War, 1914–1918—England—Fiction. 2. World War, 1914–1918—France—Fiction. 3. War—Fiction. 4. Fathers and sons—Fiction.] I. Title.
    PZ7.L43545 Lo 2001
    [Fic]—dc21
                                2001017254

The text of this book is set in 13-point Granjon.

Book design by Melissa Knight

Map by Virginia Norey

Manufactured in the United States of America

October 2001

10 9 8 7 6 5 4 3 2 1

BVG

For Kathleen

CHAPTER 1

My dad was a toy maker, the finest in London. He made miniature castles and marionettes, trams and trains and carriages. He carved a hobbyhorse that Princess Mary rode through the ballroom at Buckingham Palace. But the most wonderful thing that Dad ever made was an army of nutcracker men.

He gave them to me on my ninth birthday, thirty soldiers carved from wood, dressed in helmets and tall black boots. They carried rifles tipped with silver bayonets. They had enormous mouths full of grinning teeth that sparkled in the sun.

They were so beautiful that every boy who saw them asked for a set for himself. But Dad never made others. "They're one of a kind," he said. "Those are very special soldiers, those."

I had no other army to fight them against, so I marched my nutcracker men across the kitchen floor, flattening buildings that I made out of cards. I pretended that no other army even *dared* to fight against those fierce-looking soldiers.

When I was ten, the war started in Europe, the war they said would end all wars. The Kaiser's army stormed into Luxembourg, and all of Europe fled before it.

But for me, the war really began on the day the butcher vanished, when I found his door mysteriously locked. Inside, the huge carcasses hung on their hooks, and the rows of pink meat lay on the counters. Yet there was no sign of Fatty Dienst, who had greeted me there just the day before—as he always had—with a great smile and a laugh, with a nub of spicy sausage hidden in his apron pocket. He'd pulled it out in his hand that had no thumb, and said—as always—"*Ach,* look what I've found, Johnny." His accent turned my name into Chonny. "That's goot Cherman sausage there, Chonny," he'd told me.

That night I asked my dad, "What happened to Fatty Dienst?"

"That *butcher?*" said Dad. "I suppose he's gone home to be with all the *other* butchers. To join that *army* of butchers."

I didn't understand; they had always been friends. Many times I had seen Dad laughing at Fatty's jokes, or the German winking as he slipped an extra slice of ham in with the rest.

"I never trusted that man," said Dad.

Then the others vanished: Mr. Hoffman the barber, Henrik the shoemaker, Willy Kempf the doorman. They slipped away one by one, and soon only Siegfried was left from all the Germans I'd ever known, poor little Siegfried who worked as a waiter. I went to school with one of his sons.

But it wasn't much longer until I saw *him* leaving too,

with his wife and their children, each with a suitcase made out of cardboard. A crowd of boys and barking men drove them along like so many sheep. Some of my pals ran in circles around the poor man, who walked so slowly and sadly that I felt like crying.

Dad was watching beside me, in the window of our flat. He looked furious. "Do you know what that fellow was doing?"

"Serving people?" I asked.

"Telling them he was Swiss," said Dad, his hands clenched. "But I demanded to see his passport, and showed up the rotter for what he was."

Off they went, with their little cardboard suitcases, down toward the railway station on Victoria Street. Dad flung open the window and shouted after them, "Go along home!" It made no sense; their home was in London, just around the corner. Only the week before, I had seen Dad get up from our supper at Paddington Station and press a tanner into little Siegfried's hand. But now he seemed full of hate, and I thought I would never understand how a man could be his friend one day, and his enemy the next.

Then the Kaiser's army stormed into Belgium. I saw them at the picture show, hundreds of soldiers looking just like my nutcracker men, all in black boots and silver-tipped helmets. They flickered across the screen, their arms held stiff at their sides but their legs swinging high. They marched on and on as though nothing would stop them. And I started asking my dad, "Can you make me some Frenchmen? Can you make me some Tommies?"

There was nothing Dad wouldn't do for me. He whittled away in his shop, and came home with a tiny

Frenchman, his blue coat buttoned back into flaps, his legs marching. I named him Pierre. The next day it was a Tommy that Dad brought home, with the tiniest Union Jack I'd ever seen painted on his sleeve. I put him into the battle on the fifth day of August, 1914, the night that Britain went to war.

All of London seemed to celebrate. Men joined up by the hundreds, by the thousands, marching away in tremendous, cheering parades. They passed my father's toy shop, stepping along, singing along, as the women shouted and the children dashed in amongst them. Through a blizzard of rose petals, they passed in such numbers, with such a stamping of feet, that the smaller toys shook on my father's shelves. But Dad didn't go with them.

"Aren't you signing up?" I asked him. "Aren't you going to the war?"

"Johnny," he said, "I'm afraid the King doesn't need me just now."

We were watching them pass, the new soldiers. They were clean and smart, like freshly made toys.

"Don't you *want* to go?" I asked.

"But what about you? What about your mother?" He shook his head. "No, Johnny, I think I'm better off here. Some of us have duties at home."

"Like what?" I asked. The soldiers were still passing by.

"Well," he said, "I have to build up your little army, don't I? Someone has to stop your nutcracker men."

Already, they had captured nearly all of the kitchen. They were spilling through the parlor door, where my lone Pierre was putting up a brave fight. Then my mum stood by mistake on my army, and one of the nutcracker men got his hand broken off.

"Look what you did!" I cried.

"Oh, Johnny, I'm sorry," she said. "But do they have to be underfoot like this? Can't you play somewhere else?"

So I rushed them forward, into the parlor. And leading the charge was the man with no hand. I pretended it was Fatty Dienst. "Go forward!" he shouted as the Frenchman retreated again. "Go forward for Chermany!"

Down the street, in the little butcher shop, the meat turned gray and then brown. A horrid smell came out through the door. Someone smashed the windows; then a bobby came round and boarded them up. And the Germans kept marching, west across Flanders, rolling armies ahead of them with no more bother than my nutcracker men.

Ambulances carrying soldiers from the front went rattling past my dad's shop. People turned out to cheer them as loudly as they'd cheered the soldiers going the other way. Big advertisements appeared everywhere, enormous posters that said, "Your Country Needs You." And more parades of new soldiers marched down the streets, though Dad stayed home. He built up my little French army one man at a time.

"Is Dad a coward?" I asked my mum.

"Of course he's not," she said.

"Then why doesn't he go to the war?"

"Well, he doesn't like to say this, but he's just not tall enough, Johnny."

"Not tall enough?" He seemed like a giant to me.

"He's five foot seven," she said. "An inch too short for the King."

It made me sad that he was too short, and sad that the King didn't want him. But Dad was even sadder; he never laughed, or even smiled, as summer turned into autumn, as the war went on in France. He started flying into rages at the least little thing, and he scattered my army of nutcracker men when they came too close to his favorite chair. In Europe, the French and the British turned the Germans back at the Marne, but even that didn't cheer up Dad.

In late September he brought home a cuckoo clock that was all in pieces. "Someone smashed it," he said. "I had it in my window, and a fellow got into a fit because he thought it was German!" The little cuckoo bird dangled from a broken spring, and it chirped as Dad shook the clock. "Anyone can see that it's Swiss."

On the first of October he brought home a box of toy soldiers. They were British Tommies, little soldiers and machine gunners, cast from lead by a German toy maker.

Dad dropped the box on the floor. "You might as well have these, Johnny," he said. "No one's going to buy them now, and that's *damned* certain."

He never swore. So my mother gave him a dark look, and he turned very red.

"Well, they're not," he said. "If it comes from Germany, nobody wants it. No one will touch it, except to smash it. I saw a man go out of his way—clear across Baker Street—to kick at a dachshund a lady was walking."

"But we *are* at war," said Mum, trying to console him. "Those little lead soldiers might only be toys to you, but to other men they're something worth fighting about."

Dad scowled but didn't argue back. He sat in his chair, staring through the window at the buildings and the sky. It was just a few days later when he went off to his shop in the morning, and came home in a uniform. He had joined the British Army.

"They lowered the height!" he cried. "It's five foot five. I'll be a giant among the next batch of men."

His uniform didn't fit him very well. It drooped around him like a lot of greenish brown sacks, and the funny puttees—wound too many times round his legs—were held in place with his bicycle clips.

I laughed when I saw him like that. But Mum cried. She went at him with a mouthful of pins, tucking him all into shape like one of his little felt dolls. And all the time, as she nipped and tucked, she cried great tears that poured from her without any sound.

Dad softened his voice. "I have to do my bit. We have to lick the Germans."

He packed his things in a little bag. He sat on the floor and packed a book to read, and his carving set, his paints and inks. Mum smiled when she saw him doing that. She looked terribly sad, but she smiled. Then she bent down and kissed the top of his head.

Dad looked surprised. He gathered the rest of his things in a hurry, then stood up with his little bag. "I won't be gone for long," he said. "I'll be home in time for Christmas."

That was ten weeks away; it seemed forever.

"No tears, now," said Dad. "The time will pass before you know it." He hugged me. "I'll see you at Christmas."

He said the same thing at the railway station, and he shouted it from a window as the train started down the track. "Bye-bye, Johnny," he said. "See you at Christmas." A thousand men leaned from the windows, every one dressed in khaki, all waving their arms. They looked like a forest sliding down the platform, drawing away in blasts of steam. They left us all behind, a crowd of children and women and old, gray men. The platform was littered with rose petals.

We waved; we cheered and shouted until the train clattered across a point and the last carriage slipped around the bend. Then there was a silence that made the air seem thick and heavy. Nobody wanted to leave, but no one would look at anybody else. My mother covered her mouth with her handkerchief, took my hand, and pulled me away.

CHAPTER 2

October 25, 1914

Dearest Johnny,

We're having a grand time here at training camp. We practice falling down and getting up, and stabbing at bags of straw with our bayonets. But mostly we practice marching, round and round, with enormous packs on our backs. I'm losing a bit of weight with all the work, but I think it's mostly from my feet.

The officers are a great bunch. Very amusing. I've never met men who can shout so loudly for so long. They shouted at us this morning that we'll be off to France very soon. We're eager to have a crack at old Fritz, and the biggest fear is that the war will end before we get there.

Enclosed is one little Frenchman that I whittled in my spare time. Good luck with your battles.

> *Love,*
> *Dad*

I named my soldier Pierre Six. I had five Frenchmen already, and didn't know any other names. I put him into action with the other Pierres and the metal Tommies, battling the nutcracker men at the edge of the carpet. I called it the banks of the Aisne.

The Western Front was now a line of trenches that stretched from the Channel to the Swiss frontier. My dad had been gone for less than three weeks, but it seemed like forever. In all my life, before the war, I'd never spent as much as a day without him.

I rushed my nutcracker men across the parlor carpet. "Ratta-tatta-tatta!" I shouted as the Tommies opened fire. I screamed for the nutcracker men as they spun and fell.

"Aarrgh!" shouted Fatty Dienst. He started crawling, and I gasped his voice. "I must keep going. I must fight on for Chermany."

"Johnny!" said my mother.

I looked up at her in the doorway. She'd brought in the Browns from the flat downstairs, and they peered past her at my battlefield.

"If you have to play those games, please play them in your room," she said.

"But Fritz is on the run," I told her.

Mr. Brown laughed. He came through the door, then tugged up his trousers and squatted beside me. He was round as a football, with a round, pink head and little round spectacles. He picked up Pierre Three. "Cor," he said, like a schoolboy. "It looks quite alive." He swiveled on his heels and held the soldier toward my mum and Mrs. Brown. "Look. There's laces in his boots. It's remarkable."

Mr. Brown put the Frenchman on the carpet, then

rushed him at Fatty Dienst. The little German toppled over again. *"Mein Gott!"* gasped Mr. Brown. *"Gott in Himmel,* I'm done for."

"Honestly!" cried Mrs. Brown. "Maybe you should both go and play in Johnny's room."

I wouldn't have minded that, but Mum sent me out instead. "Go on," she said. "It's a gorgeous day."

I was glad the war was on. It made London an exciting place, with something new nearly every day. Rings of sandbags appeared in Regent's Park as suddenly and mysteriously as fairy rings. Guns popped up inside them; then soldiers appeared, as though from nowhere. Laborers arrived with lorries full of pipe and wire, and they laid a line of lampposts through the middle of the park.

I thought it was a mistake, but the soldiers said the lamps were going to fool the Kaiser when he sent his zeppelins over London. "From up there it will look like the busiest street in the city," they said. "The zepps will aim for that, and all they'll hit is grass."

The zeppelins were longer than the highest building in London, the soldiers told me. They would glide across the sky like dreadnoughts on a sea of stars.

"What will they do up there?" I asked.

"Burn," the soldiers said, and laughed. Their guns had only three or four shells each—one had none at all— but that didn't bother them. "We'll light the zepps up like fireworks. Bloody big bags of gas, that's all that zepps are, Johnny."

I was watching with Mum at the window when the lamps came on for the first time. I laughed to see a street that wasn't there; it was such a grand joke to play on the Kaiser. All around the park, the trams and carts and motorcars clattered along in a fudgy gloom because only half of the *real* lights were lit.

"I hope a zepp comes tonight," I said.

"A *zepp*," she scoffed. "Why on earth do you wish for that?"

"Because we can watch it from here," I said. "We live right beside the target."

She looked at the lights, then up at the sky. "Oh, Johnny," she whispered.

I could tell she was scared by the way her fingertips touched her lips, then trickled like water down her chin. I could *feel* that she was scared, and I tried to laugh, because adults weren't supposed to be scared.

"Don't worry, Mum," I told her. "The zepps will burn like fireworks. They're just bloody big bags—"

"Johnny!" she said.

"Of gas! That's all they are."

"Where are you learning to talk like this?" she asked. "What's happening to you, Johnny?"

She swept the curtains shut, then pulled me from the window. "I don't like it," she said. "All your army games, you and your chums running around with sticks for guns, everyone getting shot and killed."

"We don't really get killed," I told her.

"It's a wonder," said Mum. "It's a miracle you haven't taken out somebody's eye." She wrung her hands together. "It's too much, Johnny."

She ran into the kitchen. I heard a splash of water, and when she came back, her face was wet and bright from scrubbing. Her eyes were very red. "Johnny," she said. "Do you remember your Auntie Ivy?"

"Prickly Ivy?" I asked.

A little twitch started at her mouth, but she was too serious to smile. "She's your father's sister," she said. "I don't think he'd be happy to hear that from you."

She took my hands and sat again, holding me in front of her. "Your auntie lives in Cliffe. Out in the country. You could go and stay with her for a while. Just until Christmas, of course. Just until the war is over." She stared into my eyes. "How would you like that, Johnny?"

"Not much," I said.

But it didn't matter what I thought. Mum sent off some letters and a telegram, and before I knew it I was on my way to Cliffe. I spent a sad day going around the streets and through the park, saying goodbye to my friends and the soldiers at the guns. I said goodbye to the animals in the zoo, to the squirrels and the rabbits that came and gathered around me, as they'd always done. I patted Black Charlie, the ragman's huge horse, and fed him one last piece of barley sugar.

Then my mum packed my clothes, and I packed my soldiers, my beautiful nutcracker men, all my Pierres, and my little army of metal Tommies. We walked through the city, over London Bridge to Victoria Station. It was the same route that Siegfried had taken, and I was frightened that people would think we were German, that they would shout at us and drive us along.

"Should we sing 'God Save the King'?" I asked.

"I don't feel like singing," said Mum.

We walked very slowly, stopping to watch a dustman empty the bins, and again to see a chimney sweep's brush poke up from somebody's flue in a cloud of black soot. Mum talked about Cliffe, and how she and my dad had met on the train.

"I was working at Woolwich," she said. "At the arsenal. One day I got on the train to go into London, and I sat beside a handsome man. The nicest man."

"My dad?" I asked.

"That's right."

I switched hands on my suitcase. "How did you know that he was my dad?"

"Well, he wasn't then. Not yet," she said. "I was certain he was a barrister or something. He looked so important, with his little briefcase on his lap. What a shock I got when he opened it. There were puppets in there, and he made them sit up and talk to me."

We were both laughing when we came to the station. I had forgotten how sad I was, until Mum left me at the platform gates and went to buy my ticket. She had to push through a crowd to get there, then push her way back. She knelt in front of me. "You look so grown up," she said. "Such a little man."

She straightened my tie, smiling and crying at the same time. People were passing us, queuing up at the gate where the man punched their tickets. I could hear steam hissing from the train on the platform.

"Now, listen," said Mum. "You'll pass Beckley Hill and Buckland Farm, and the next stop will be Cliffe. Your Auntie Ivy will meet you at the station."

The train whistled. I heard the clicking of the man's ticket puncher. Someone cried, "All aboard!"

"Go," said Mum. She hugged me and kissed me. "You'd better go."

I picked up my suitcase and dragged the other one. The man took my ticket. "Hurry, son," he said.

Mum was standing on her toes, her arm reaching. "Johnny, I love you," she shouted, and the crowd closed between us. Compartment doors were slamming shut up and down the train. A fat man all in black crashed against me. A lady knocked a suitcase from my hand. "Mum!" I said.

A Highlander in his kilt and green stockings picked up my suitcase. He took the other one from me—both in one arm—and clamped a huge fist on my shoulder. "You poor laddie," he shouted. "Don't you fret. I'll see you settled, all right."

The train shrieked and puffed. It jerked forward with a bang of couplers. The Highlander pulled me with him, in through the door of the nearest compartment. The train jolted again, and we fell together onto the seat. Someone reached past me and closed the door, and the train steamed out of the station.

The compartment was barely half full. Only six people sat on the benches that stretched across the width of the train. The Highlander bent down and lifted my suitcases onto the seat. He pretended to groan at their weight. "Och, what have you got in there?" he asked in his great, loud voice.

I showed him all my soldiers. When he saw the Pierres he winked. "Their feet are on backwards," he said.

"They're not," I told him.

"But the Frenchies never go frontwards," he roared, winking furiously.

There was something odd about him. He sat for a while, glowering through the window, then suddenly shouted again. "Where did you get the wee soldiers?"

"From my father," I said.

"Eh? Your father?" His face pulsed with a violent twitch. "You're on your way to see him?"

"No," I said. "He's in the army. He's going to France."

"Eh?"

He was deaf as a post. I shouted back, "He's going to the front!"

"Is he?" shouted the Highlander.

"Yes. I won't see him until Christmas."

"Don't you believe it," the Highlander bellowed. "You won't see him for years to come."

The other people in the compartment were tilted toward us, frowning as they listened. The Highlander kept winking in his ghastly way. I didn't think he even knew he was doing it.

"We'll never win this war," he said. "It can't be done."

An angry man, the fat one all in black, told him not to talk such rubbish. The Highlander whirled toward him, twitching horribly. "I was there," he said, even more loudly. "I watched the Frenchies streaming past and saw the Huns come thick as eels, squirming over the mud and the ground, all their guns ablaze." He winked and shouted. "I was there at Loos, in a field of corpses. We marched shoulder to shoulder against the Germans, until they got so sick of killing us that they turned their guns aside."

"You're off your head," said the man in black. And a woman beside him said, "He's daft."

The Highlander laughed. "Aye, there's some that call it daft. I call it common sense." He winked and twitched at the faces. "Well, I'm no going back," he roared. "Och, I'll never go back to there."

"You're a coward, then," said the angry man.

Again the Highlander laughed. "Why aren't you at the front?"

The angry man blushed. The whole compartment was suddenly staring at *him,* and he seemed to shake in his seat as the train swayed along the tracks. "I've got a family," he said. "A wife and children."

"Och, so do I," said the Highlander. "I've got a laddie just like this one here." He touched my back. "He'll be an old man before this war is done. An old, gray man he'll be."

There was a woman sitting beside him, and she got up then and moved away. A man slid out from the opposite seat; another woman followed him. Suddenly there was a big, empty space around the Highlander and me. And someone came and plucked me out, until only the Highlander was left, like a little island.

"I was there." He sat winking and twitching, staring ahead. "I tell you, I was there."

Chapter 3

October 30, 1914

Dearest Johnny,

I am writing in a great rush. We are packing our kits. It's off to France!

I can't help but marvel how lucky I was to join the regular army instead of Kitchener's bunch. All those men who signed up before me are parading around in the streets and the parks. Most of them are still in their civilian clothes, and many are drilling with sticks instead of rifles. Poor chaps; for all their eagerness they'll get to France long after me. I shouldn't be surprised if we have the job finished before the first of them crosses the Channel.

This is the last you will hear from me until I am up at the front.

I hope you are happy in Cliffe.

Enclosed, one drill sergeant to boss us about. Also enclosed, one general to boss the sergeant about.

> *Love,*
> *Dad*

The letter was waiting at Auntie's when I came in from my first day at school. There was another from Mum, and Auntie Ivy had opened them both.

"Will you read them?" I asked.

"Aloud?" said Auntie. "Can't you read for yourself?"

"Not these," I said.

Dad wrote in slanted letters full of little curls and loops. They looked like rows of fancy birds perched on invisible wires. Mum's were even worse; they didn't even look like letters at all. They were more like bits of string tangled into coils and tiny knots.

"Well, honestly," said Auntie. She put on the daintiest spectacles I'd ever seen, just circles of glass joined by a wire. They pinched across her sharp little nose, fitting perfectly into little red dents that seemed to be there just to hold her specs. "Which one first?"

"Mum's," I said.

Auntie started reading. I closed my eyes.

" 'The place seems empty without you,' " read Auntie. " 'I miss seeing you and hearing you, and I even miss your little soldiers being scattered all about. But I'm so glad you're in Cliffe, Johnny, because London isn't a place for a boy anymore. At night it's blacked out, and it feels scary and wild. Every time I hear a motorcar go by I look up, sure that it's a zeppelin.' "

Auntie Ivy shook her head. "Imagine," she said, and started reading again.

"Men are still signing up in hordes," wrote Mum. "But no one is hiring women to fill their posts. It's very maddening, as there is so much that I could do to help. Unless something changes, I may have to go back to my old job at the arsenal in Woolwich. It's a dreadful place, but at least I would be closer to you."

I sat in my school clothes—or most of them—still sodden from the rain. Auntie Ivy folded up my mother's letter and read the one from my father. I waited until she finished before I unwrapped my soldiers.

"Oh, look!" I cried.

The general was stiff and proper, with a little swagger stick clamped under his arm. The drill sergeant was nearly his opposite, short and stout, his chest barreling like a strongman's. He wore a tiny cap atop a huge head that was nearly entirely an open, bellowing mouth. I could look right down his throat at little tonsils painted like pink hearts.

Auntie laughed, and that took me by surprise. I knew she could shout, and I knew she could look daggers with her little dark eyes, but I didn't know that she could laugh.

"I'll call the general Cedric," I said.

"That's lovely," she said. "He looks like a Cedric. Now take them outside."

"It's raining," I said.

"A little rain never hurt a boy." She took off her specs and rubbed her nose. "You're not made of sugar, are you?"

"No, Auntie," I said.

"Then don't be so silly. You know the rules."

She didn't let me play soldiers in the house. It wasn't right, she said—it wasn't "fitting"—to bring war inside a house. But there were a lot of things that Auntie Ivy didn't like: sudden noises, elbows on the table, the banging of doors, and mindless chatter. "I can't *abide* mindless chatter," she'd told me.

Now she stood up. "Well, off you go," she said. "I've got Christmas socks to knit for the boys at the front."

She wore big black shoes that thunked when she walked, and purple dresses that touched the floor. Forever after, I would think of Auntie Ivy as a sound, as the thunk of her shoes and the swish of her legs in the heavy cloth.

"Go on now," she said as she passed.

"Yes, Auntie," I said.

I hated her rules—and her house that was drafty and cold. I hated the school, and I hated the teacher, and I hated the boys most of all. They had teased me because I'd carried my things in a satchel, because I'd worn my blazer and flannel shorts. They'd called me Johnny Pigs instead of Briggs, and they'd pushed me down and sat on my head. The teacher—ugly old Mr. Tuttle—had only looked toward us, then looked away. The only person who was nice to me was a girl, and that was almost as bad as not having a friend at all.

Well, I wasn't going back. Auntie Ivy didn't know it, but I'd never go back. "Oh, there's some that call it daft," I muttered to myself. "But *I* call it common sense."

I hated almost *everything* about Cliffe: the mile-long walk to the village; the flatness without any buildings. I felt lonely without my mother and my father. I missed my pals from London: even the soldiers at their guns.

But then there was Auntie Ivy's garden, nearly the size of our whole London home. It sloped up at the back, toward a stone wall and a huge beech tree that poked its roots right through the stones. All the leaves had fallen long ago, but the bare branches were enough to stop most of the rain. And in the mud below them, I scraped out trenches in the sloping ground. I put the British in one, the Frenchmen on their right, and in the other I put the Germans. I crowded them together, all my lovely nut-cracker men. I still had many more Germans than anything else.

I arranged them carefully. And when the ground was covered with soldiers I heard a voice behind me. "Hello, Johnny."

It was Sarah, the girl from school. She was carrying my satchel, and beside her stood a tall lieutenant in a Burberry coat. "This is my father," she said. "He's on his way to the station. He's leaving for France."

"*My* dad's already left for France," I said.

"Well, *mine's* been there and back," said Sarah, gloating. "He's home on leave, that's all."

The lieutenant said, "Hello. Johnny, is it?" He smiled at me, then looked down at my soldiers.

"I brought you this," said Sarah, holding out my satchel. "You forgot it at school."

I hadn't forgotten it. I had stuffed it down behind the steps, too embarrassed to ever use it again. "I don't want it," I said.

"Can I have it?" she asked.

I shrugged. "All right."

The lieutenant was crouched over my nutcracker men. "Look at these, Sarah," he said. "They're beautiful soldiers."

"They look so fierce," she said.

"That's because they're Huns," I told her.

The lieutenant's coat was unbuttoned, spreading behind him across the mud. "Your trenches are too far apart, Johnny," he said. "You've got the Germans running across a mile of ground." He waved his hand above the soldiers. "It should be less than a hundred yards; perhaps just twenty-five."

I looked down at my trenches, already filling with rain. One of the wooden Pierres was floating on his side.

"Move them closer," said Sarah's dad. "Move your Tommies forward."

"They'll be right on top of my Germans," I said.

"Yes. That's the idea. They should be close enough that they can sometimes hear the Germans talking." He sketched a line through the mud of my no-man's-land. "Dig a new trench here, and leave the old one behind it, so your Tommies have somewhere to hide when they're driven back."

"They won't be driven back," I said.

"Oh, yes they will," he told me.

I scraped out a new trench, and Sarah helped me move the soldiers. With her left hand holding her dress, she bent down and lifted the men one at a time, like flowers she was picking. No girl had ever touched my soldiers, and it didn't seem right. A boy would have made them fight, but Sarah only moved them around like so many dolls. Then her father joined us, and we worked together below the great umbrella of the beech tree.

When all the soldiers were in their places, the lieutenant studied my battlefield. "You'll have to build communication trenches so your men can move up to the front," he said. "Otherwise your Germans will pick them off as they cross the top. You want your Tommies to live in the earth."

"Like moles?" I asked.

"Exactly." He squinted at the trenches. "Your general, now. That won't do where you've got him."

I stared down at little Cedric standing with the rest of the Tommies. "He's right at the front," I said.

"That's what I mean. He's in the wrong place altogether." The lieutenant stood up. "You should move him back. That's where he'd really be."

I picked up the little man and set him in the rear trench.

"Farther," said the lieutenant. "You have to move him back so far that he can't see the battles. Then move him a little more, so he can think he's winning them when he's not."

Sarah giggled. "That's silly," she said.

"It's the way it is," said her father with a shrug. "Well, I've got a train to catch. Sarah, would you like to stay here with your chum?"

I looked at Sarah, to see that she was looking at me. I didn't mind her being in the garden; I didn't even mind her touching my soldiers. But I didn't ask her to stay, and both of us looked down at the ground.

The lieutenant laughed. "Perhaps you'd rather see me off at the station."

Sarah went with him, into the mist of rain. I felt a pang of jealousy to see her walking at his side, with my satchel on her shoulder. She called back from the house: "I'll see you at school."

I didn't tell her I was finished with school.

In the morning Auntie Ivy sent me off in my boots and macintosh. I trudged up the road to Cliffe, past an orchard and a farm, past a cottage and a field. When I saw the big, square steeple of the village church I turned off the road, skirting the houses and the school to reach the marshes by the Thames.

I spent all morning there. I watched a Bristol aeroplane and an Albatros in British colors flying down the river to Grain. I ran through the long grass, scaring up herons that squawked into the air like clumsy old Bleriots. And I pretended to dogfight with them, running across the humps of ground with my arms stretched out like wings.

In the afternoon I went exploring along footpaths as the rain pattered down on my mac. I gathered sticks as I went along, because it was already the third of November, and the fifth was Guy Fawkes Day. I wished more than ever that I was back in London, for all my pals would be making their guys, stuffing sacks full of leaves and twigs, shaping them into arms and legs and bodies, dressing the figures in old clothes. They would wheel them through the city, collecting pennies to buy their fireworks. On Guy Fawkes Day they would light a huge bonfire and dance around it, then toss the sad old guys onto the flames. Except for Christmas, that was my favorite day of the year.

But the rain had fallen for so long in Kent that all the leaves were rotting and all the sticks were too wet to burn. I searched along the footpaths until I found a rabbit's tunnel through a hedge and squirmed along it, into a wonderful, secret garden.

Against the walls of a thatched-roof cottage lay piles of thorny branches, all clipped and dry. In a little greenhouse were empty sacks and a great bag of mulch just waiting for a boy to come along and take. At the back of the garden, beside a stack of planks at a short bit of wall, grew a wild tangle of bushes that were thorny at the top but smooth at the bottom. I tore whole branches away.

I was hardly able to squeeze through the hedge with all I'd found. It was enough to make the biggest guy in Cliffe; the biggest guy in the whole world. The boys would like me then, I thought.

But I had to be crafty about it. I dragged the sacks along the footpaths and hid them behind the wall at Auntie's garden. I waited for the sounds of school ending for the day—the bell and the shrieks of children. Then I waited a bit longer before I went home.

Poor Auntie Ivy felt so sorry for me that she gave me cocoa with a spoonful of Horlicks. "Honestly," she said. "I don't understand how a boy can get so wet and so muddy just walking home from school."

"It was raining awfully hard in the village," I said, sly as a fox.

"A parcel came," she said. "Something from your father."

CHAPTER 4

October 31, 1914

Dearest Johnny,

We hopped across the Channel yesterday morning and got to the front in time for tea. Well, not quite to the front, though it's amazing how close the battle is to home.

When we got off the train, I heard the guns for the first time. Still very faint, they made little whumps, like someone plumping at a pillow. I could see flashes of light, low to the ground. In the rain and clouds it looked like a thunderstorm brewing.

Fritz has made a proper mess of everything here. There are buildings that he has blasted apart. Some, just the chimneys are standing. There is a steady stream of people heading west, pushing all their belongings in wheelbarrows. We marched past them all night long, through a rainstorm, through mud like you wouldn't believe.

Where a farmer had his field, it's mud. Where a village stood, it's mud. If it weren't for the crumbled heaps of stone, here and there a shattered tree, you'd think there'd never been anything else but mud. It swallows up the horses, and it swallows up the other horses that come to pull them out. I saw three dead ones standing in a row, looking as though they were grazing, but stuck like flies to paper. I saw a huge cannon buried up to its barrel, and twenty poor lads trying to get it loose.

And the rain. Why, Johnny, it never stops. I think they might have told us about the rain, and I could have brought my umbrella. Sixty pounds I have to carry on my poor old back, so how much harder would it have been to bring a brolly?

At any rate, I'm in the rear trenches now. We'll be moving up in two or three days, when the lads at the front are ready for a rest. A week after that I'll be back here myself. I have to say that it sounds like quite an easy life, all in all.

Enclosed, for your British Army, one little soldier. Ask your auntie who it is.

> *All my love,*
> *Dad*

Wrapped in old paper was the smallest man that Dad had ever made. Brightly painted, with a grin on his face and a silver tag on his wrist, he wore a British uniform, a smart new jacket. He carried a funny little rifle too tiny for his hands, like a toy soldier with a toy gun of his own. He was rooted in mud that bubbled round his boots and puttees like lumps of pudding.

"Who is it, Auntie?" I asked.

"I don't feel like playing games," said Auntie. But she aimed her spectacles toward the little soldier. "How should I know who it is?"

I stood the figure on the table. Auntie Ivy leaned closer. "Oh, for mercy's sake," she said.

"What?" I asked.

"Johnny, that's your father." Her laughter reminded me of the geese in Regent's Park. "That's his old toy gun, that little gun. He was forever playing with that."

I looked at the soldier, and saw tiny bicycle clips painted round his puttees.

Auntie Ivy took off her spectacles. She laughed again, her silver hair wobbling. "Who but your father would sit in the trenches as the guns went off, carving a model of himself?"

"I'm going to put him in the line," I said. "Then I'm going to build a guy."

"What about your schoolwork?" asked Auntie.

"Oh, I don't have any today." Slyly, I added, "I don't think I *ever* will."

I put the model in the rear trench, just where my real dad had been when he'd written his letter. Across no-man's-land, the nutcracker men watched with their fierce stares. I wanted to send my dad marching against them, but I had to build my communication trenches.

I gouged them out, joining the front lines to the rear. The handfuls of mud became artillery shells, and I tossed them high in the air. I said it was a German barrage, and I made whistling sounds, and booms, as the mud rained down on my men.

"Whoosh. Bang!" Dirt splattered across the soldiers. The little figures leaned, then fell, as though cowering into the dirt.

"Quickly, now!" I ran my new soldier up to the front.

He twisted through the communication trench as bullets whizzed around him. "Bang, bang!" I shouted, jabbing at the mud. He ducked and carried on, up to the front with the others. I took the drill sergeant and turned him toward my father. "You're here," he bellowed. "Good show, Private Briggs!"

I left him there and went away to build my guy. I pestered Auntie Ivy for stockings to make the arms and legs, for string to tie them all together. I crammed them full of branches, then pestered her for clothes.

"Honestly," she said. "Will this never stop?"

"But I have to dress my guy," I said.

She clucked her tongue. "I suppose I might have an old skirt you can have."

"A *skirt?*" I cried. "I can't dress my guy in a skirt."

"Can't you pretend that all the men guys are up at the front?"

"No, Auntie. That wouldn't do."

"All *right,*" she said. "For heaven's sake." She took me through the house and up the stairs, her enormous shoes clunking like artillery. "I don't know why you can't leave me in peace."

We went to the room at the back of the house. It was full of old furniture and a jumble of boxes. In the corner was a steamer trunk, and Auntie Ivy swept away the blankets and the bedsheets piled on top. She flicked the latches open.

"These were your father's things," she said. "I suppose you can take what you need."

I wanted the most wonderful guy, the biggest and best of any. But the clothes in the chest were the ones my father had worn as a boy, and they were too small for my overstuffed sacks and stockings. When I finished, I sat and cried. The guy looked like a monster that had suddenly grown from a boy himself, exploding from his shorts and cardigan. The cloth cap balanced like a button on the top of his gigantic head.

"It's quite grand," said Auntie Ivy when I showed her.

"It's silly." I gave the thing a kick in the chest. "He looks like Tweedledum."

It was too late then to take my guy to the village. The next morning it was too chancy, because I should have been in school. So I left him in the potting shed, sprawled among the garden canes, and went back to the marshes.

The day was cold and drizzly. I walked for miles and never saw a soul, and hours had never seemed longer. Finally, I trekked back to the village and sat on the step at the post office, sheltered from the rain by its overhanging floors.

As I waited for the school bell, I heard hooves plodding on the road. Around a corner came the postman, rumbling down the street in his one-horse van. He wore a rubber cape folded back across his head, and didn't see me sitting on his bench. He tossed down the big mailbags that he'd brought from the station, then dragged them to the door. But he stopped when he came up beside me.

"What are you doing?" he asked.

"Waiting," I said.

He was a kindly old geezer. He sat down beside me. "Where's your mother?" he asked.

"In London," I said.

"And your father?"

"At the front."

"Oh, you poor child." He looked close to tears. "Here you are, dressed up like a lord. And you're only a poor little waif." He patted my knee. "But never you mind. You come in and get warm."

"Thank you, sir," I said.

The postman had a little office at the back of his building, and we sat in there, between a cast-iron stove and a table that held boxes and pens and a telegraph key. He put a kettle on to boil, then gave me a roast beef sandwich that was wrapped in greasy paper. "When was the last time you ate?" he asked.

"This morning," I said. "My auntie made me breakfast."

He looked at me, then laughed. "Who's your auntie, son?"

"Ivy Briggs," I told him.

"Ah, you're Johnny then. The boy who gets packages that I have to carry, don't I?" He pretended to shake his fist at me. Then he smiled and said, "Why aren't you in school?"

"I don't like it there," I said.

"Ah. So you've come out here so your aunt will think you're there." He pushed back in his chair. "Well, you're James Briggs's son all right, that's for certain. Many a day I found him sitting in one place when he was supposed to be at another."

"Really?" I said.

"Oh, Lord yes." He got up to see to his kettle. "Usually I'd find him out at the station. He was mad about trains, your father. Quite the spotter; keen as mustard."

I laughed at that, my father watching trains. I only knew that he complained all the time about the noise and smoke they made.

"Yes, keen as mustard," the postman said again, as though he hoped I would laugh a second time.

A bell rang then, a sharp jangle that made the old postman jump. "Oh, Lord," he said. "Here's another one."

"Another what?" I asked.

"Another broken heart." He leaned over the table and clamped a set of earphones on his head. He closed his eyes for a moment, took up a pencil, and started jotting letters on a pad of paper. His letters became words, his words a sentence. Then he tapped a few times on his telegraph key, took off his earphones, and folded the paper.

"Yes, it's another lad gone," he said, with a heavy sigh. "Another soldier who won't be home."

He put his paper in an envelope. "I'd better be off," he told me. "Crikey. It's a blasted job being a messenger for cold Mr. Death."

He put on his cape and a pillbox hat, and went out again to the drizzle. This time I went with him, around to the side of the building.

"What happened?" I asked. "Did a soldier get killed?"

"Another one, yes. 'Died of his wounds,' " he said. "That's five for little Cliffe since the war began."

There was a bicycle leaning against the wall, below the cables and wires that came in from the telegraph poles. It was covered with rust, from the pedals to the little round bell on the handlebars. When the postman climbed onto the saddle, his feet sat flat on the ground. "Do you want a lift home?" he asked.

"No, thank you," I said.

"Go to school, son. It's where a boy belongs." He pushed himself forward, put his feet on the pedals, and wobbled away on his journey. The bell, when he rang it, sounded just like the one in his office.

I looked up at the wires, tracing them from pole to pole as far as I could see. I wondered if they stretched somehow all the way to France, to the trenches and the battlefields. Then I wondered who sat at the other end, sending the news of soldiers dying. I had an image of cold Mr. Death in a black hood and black robes, tapping away with his skeleton fingers.

I was frightened that the office bell would ring again, jangling through the empty building. It would summon me into the little room, and I would put on those earphones. What would I hear? A voice: a creaky old voice? "Died of his wounds," it would say, and whisper a name.

I hurried away. My feet pattered on the road, over mud and through puddles. I ran and ran along the footpath, until I heard a scream that stopped me cold. Only once had I heard a sound like that, when a dog had been crushed by the wheels of a coach. But those cries had ended quickly, and this went on and on.

I was close enough to the little cemetery to see the tombstones standing among heaps of khaki-colored leaves. They were ringed by trees with twisted branches, like old umbrellas that the wind had torn apart. Beyond them was the farmhouse, the home of old Storey Sims.

Square and white, with an upstairs balcony facing toward me, it looked like a tombstone itself.

The screams were coming from there.

A door opened, a slit of darkness on the whitewashed wall, and out came the postman with his cap in his hands. He put it on, mounted his bicycle, and went trundling down the lane.

The cries never stopped. Around the cemetery the trees shivered, and a flurry of leaves—nearly the last—fell down among the graves. The sounds made *me* shiver too; they turned me to ice inside as I ran along the path. I wished more than ever that my mum would be waiting at home. It was the worst thing of all that Auntie Ivy was there, her sharp little nose poking into my business.

"Auntie!" I shouted, as I barged through the door. "I heard someone screaming outside."

She didn't even care. "Where have you been?" she asked.

"At school," I lied. "But, Auntie—"

"And how was school today?" Her little eyes squinted. "How was Mr. Tuttle?"

"Fine," I said. "But—"

"Oh, really? Come into the parlor, Johnny." She turned her back and went thumping down the hall.

I followed her with a fear in my stomach, a dread of what I would find. On the table by the doorway were letters from my mum and dad, but I barely glanced at those. Sitting in the rocking chair, his legs crossed at the ankles, was the last man in the world I wanted to see.

"Well?" said Auntie Ivy. "Now you can tell *Mr. Tuttle* about your fine day at school."

He sat as still as a cat that had spotted a mouse. He watched me in that same way, as though he would pounce if I tried to run. The black gown that he'd worn in class was folded over his lap. His hands rested on it, his long fingers touching at their tips. "Hello, Johnny," he said.

His face was lumpy and wrinkled, like a squash that had lain in the field through the winter. The backs of his hands were covered with scratches. Very slowly, he started flexing his fingers, and his hands moved together and then apart, like a heart beating on his lap. "You've missed two days of school," he said.

"Johnny, you're wicked," said Auntie Ivy.

Mr. Tuttle's hands kept pulsing. "No excuses?" he asked. "I expect to see you in my classroom tomorrow."

"And you will!" cried Auntie Ivy. "I'll drag him by the ear if I have to."

I cringed at the thought of that, of what the boys would say to see my auntie with me, as though I was still in infant school. "I'll be there, sir," I said.

"Excellent," said Mr. Tuttle. "We're reading the classics now; I imagine you're acquainted with Homer?"

"Homer who?" I asked.

He blinked. "The poet, Johnny."

"No, sir," I said.

"Gracious." His fingers beat faster. "Well, never mind. I live just down the road, and you can come and see me one evening a week—on Wednesdays, say—and Saturdays, of course. I shall tutor you in the classics, and get you caught up by the end of the term."

"Yes, sir," I said. My few days of freedom had cost a terrible price.

"We'll begin next Saturday," said Mr. Tuttle, rising from his chair.

Auntie Ivy gave me a black look, and went with him to the door.

I fetched my letters and waited for Auntie to read them.

CHAPTER 5

November 2, 1914

Dearest Johnny,

I like to think that I've never lied to you before, but once I did. It was just a little lie, but you caught me at it—do you remember? At that moment, when I saw the look in your eyes, I promised myself that I would never lie to you again.

Well, right now it's very hard. I think of you there in the house where I grew up and see you as a child playing beneath that enormous tree. I want so badly to tell you that everything is fine, that I'm having a splendid adventure, and that you shouldn't worry in the slightest about me. But then I remember that you're ten years old now, not really a child at all, though not quite yet a man. And it wouldn't be fair to you or me to tell you simple things like that.

The truth is, Johnny, that I'm crouched in the mud like an animal, and the man at my side is crying and holding himself, and there is nothing between us and the Boche but fifty yards of the most haunted ground I have ever imagined. I have seen it only in the flashes of star shells, but it looks even worse for that, I think. In the fizzly light of the flares it is utterly white or utterly black, with no shadows in between.

We came up to the line in a great rush, in the dead of night, running through the mud with our rifles and our packs. It is now the hour before the dawn. Old Fritz's guns are hammering at our trenches, and ours are battering his. The shells pass overhead with eerie ripping sounds, as though the sky is shredding into pieces. His guns twinkle far ahead, and ours flash behind us. But in the middle there is darkness, until a star shell bursts and flutters down. Then we see the ground heaving up, the dirt and mud all tossed about, and it looks like the Channel on a windy day, the earth a stormy sea.

The sound is tremendous. It shakes the air.

As you might suppose, I haven't had much sleep. I've spent the night carving a little officer, enclosed. It will be up to him to lead us over the top when we march against old Fritz.

The lads think I have nerves of steel to sit here carving and painting. But I find it rather relaxing.

I have to hurry now, as in just a few minutes we'll get the order to stand to. I don't know yet what the day will bring, but it can't be worse than the darkness.

I miss you very much.

> *All my love,*
> *Dad*

It was like a story cut off at the wrong place, with the ending not quite there. I was left feeling funny inside, proud and worried and sad all at once. I held the wad of crumpled paper that had come in the parcel, feeling the shape of the little man inside. I didn't want to open it.

"Read the letter again," I said.

"You just heard it," said Auntie.

"Please?" I said.

"No, Johnny. Even if I wanted to, you don't deserve it. Not after the lies you've just told me." She read the one from my mother. It talked about soldiers drilling in Hyde Park, and the suffragettes' battle to find work for women. But I barely listened.

I heard the guns in my mind. I saw the earth flying up, and my dad whittling away, his wood chips scattering. He might have been talking about the same battle I'd had in the garden as I'd moved the wooden man with his tiny gun right up to the front.

I worked at the crumpled paper until the new soldier fell out. It was a lieutenant, just like Sarah's father, wrapped in a trench coat spotted with painted mud. At his neck hung a whistle, a little tube of silver.

Auntie Ivy finished Mum's letter. "Now off you go, Johnny," she said. "And I don't want to see you until supper."

"Can I take my guy to Cliffe?" I asked.

"If you're back in an hour. If you stay away from the farm."

I didn't even *want* to go there. "I heard someone screaming," I said. "I tried to tell you, but you wouldn't listen."

"Then you shouldn't have come in telling lies."

"What happened, Auntie?" I asked. "I saw the postman there."

"He brought a telegram to Mr. and Mrs. Sims, Johnny. Murdoch, their son, just died in France." She got up from the table, and gathered her knitting. "Mr. Tuttle met the postman, who told him all about it. The Simses thought their boy was coming home. They'd been told as much. Murdoch had been wounded in the leg, and he was coming home. That was the last his parents heard, until the wire came today."

She was holding the wool and her needles, but she put them down again. "Screaming, was she? Oh, it's dreadful. Johnny, I'll walk with you as far as the farm."

I didn't have a cart or a wagon. I had to drag my guy along the road, through dirt and patches of mud. His little cloth cap fell off as he tumbled behind me. Then a leg dropped away, and Auntie Ivy carried the pieces until we reached the gates of Storey's farm.

"Don't dally," she told me. "And be sure you stop at the next house. That's where Mr. Tuttle lives."

Auntie Ivy went up to the farm, and I lugged my guy to Mr. Tuttle's house. I propped him against the hedge, put his cap in place, and chanted my little song:

"Remember remember the fifth of November,
Gunpowder treason and plot
We see no reason why this merry season
Should ever be forgot."

Mr. Tuttle appeared from the back of his house, and I shouted out, "A penny for the guy!"

He didn't come any closer. "Johnny?" he asked.

"Yes, sir," I said.

"Come to the garden."

He led me there, round the side of his house. "Look at this," he said. "Look at my roses."

I felt an awful thump in my heart to see his garden again, the same one I had found from the footpaths. It was Mr. Tuttle's roses that had stuffed my monstrous guy.

"I'm trying to save what I can," he said, going straight to the bushes. He pulled the branches apart. "See how they're splintered? The frost will get in there, and the mulch that might have kept them warm is gone."

Mr. Tuttle let the bushes snap together. He stood up. "I'm livid," he said. "I've never been more angry. These roses are all I have; they're like children to me."

I hung my head.

"Do you know who did this?"

My heart, which had sunk, fluttered again to think he didn't suspect me. "No, sir," I mumbled.

"Well, it's no concern of yours. You only came to get a penny for your guy."

I couldn't let him see it. The thorns of his roses stuck out from every part of the guy. "You don't have to give me a penny," I said.

"Nonsense," said Mr. Tuttle. He groped through his pockets and pulled out a florin. It was riches to me, twenty-four times what I'd asked for. "I'll give you this if you can tell me why I should."

I thought it was obvious. "Because I have to buy fireworks," I said.

He smiled, and I felt sorry for him. "But why, Johnny? What's the story behind the fireworks and guys?"

"Treason and plot?" I guessed.

He could tell I didn't know, but pretended that I might. "Indeed," he said. "Guy Fawkes was a Catholic, wasn't he? He hated James the First, the Protestant King, and tried to blow up the Parliament buildings on the day that all the Lords and all the Commons and the King himself would be there. But he was caught, wasn't he? He was arrested in the coal cellar with his barrels full of powder, ready to set them off on November fifth. He was hanged for treason, as you say." Mr. Tuttle held out his hand. "There you go."

I stared at the silver coin pinched in his fingers. I'd rarely owned a shilling, let alone a florin. But something inside me wouldn't let me take it. "I didn't really know," I admitted.

"You do now." He pressed the coin in my palm. "I wish all the boys were as honest as you, Johnny."

I felt miserable.

"Now, don't fret about my roses. Perhaps I can still save something."

I went on to the village, though not as cheerily as before. I sat by the Victoria Inn, with the gangly guy leaning against the wall like an old boozer, and the men smiled and the ladies giggled as they passed. I looked up at them all, shouting, "Pennies for the guy!"

All I got was a grubby old farthing, one penny and a ha'penny. Then I dragged my guy to the hardware store and went in to buy my fireworks. I asked for rockets.

"Rockets?" said the old geezer inside. "Are you mad, boy? Don't you know there's a war going on?"

"But it's Guy Fawkes Day," I said.

"No rockets. No Catherine wheels. It's only what's left over from last year, and the best of it's gone already."

43 ❖

I went away with two whizz-bangs and an old, bent tube of Crimson Rain, feeling as though all my joy in the day ahead had vanished in Mr. Tuttle's garden.

In the morning I started school again. I walked through the village, kicking at stones, and Sarah caught me up at the post office. She came too suddenly for me to go a different way, and though I tried to keep ahead of her, she could walk very fast for a girl. She skipped along at my side with my satchel on her shoulder, and the boys teased me in all new ways to see us arrive together at the school.

They shouted, "Sarah's got a boyfriend!" And, "Johnny's going to get maaaa-ried!"

In class, Mr. Tuttle singled me out for his questions about history and geography. He glowed when I knew the answers and coached me when I didn't, but I wished he would just leave me alone. I didn't want the boys to think that he liked me or, worse, to think I was smart.

When school finally ended, I was first out the door. I ran all the way home, frightened the boys would chase me.

CHAPTER 6

November 3, 1914

Dearest Johnny,

I have to admit that the front is not quite what I'd expected. To call the line a trench is rather kind. It's really just a ditch scraped through the mud, filled to my ankles with foul, brown water. All the dirt is piled behind us and before us, at the edge of a no-man's-land that's even worse in daylight than it is in darkness. Flat, black, broken by shells, it is divided by coils of barbed wire that glisten in the sun, going on and on as far as I can see.

Scattered across this no-man's-land lie men who seem to be sleeping, all flung about in the mud. A leg pokes up from here, a head from there. Yet not one of them moves, not from hour to hour or day to day, until the wind breathes across them, and their tattered clothes flap mournfully. In a funny way, I think of them as survivors, the last of the great armies that battled back and forth in the days and weeks before I came. The Huns attacked repeatedly all along this sector, and twice they captured the trench where I sit, only to be driven back within an hour or two. So the ground has been churned and churned again, until all sorts of things are buried in it now.

The smell, I have to tell you, is atrocious. And the rats can give you shivers. We have to share the trench with an army of them, a gruesome brown army that spends the days huddled in our hiding holes, in our kits and blankets. When darkness comes, they go swarming over the top to forage through the night across that dreadful no-man's-land that haunts my every dream.

The blessing is that I seldom see it. I'd rather thought that we would be fighting one long battle. That when we weren't fighting we might be playing billiards in the dugouts, or singing songs by firesides. But we stand with our guns in the morning, and again in the evening, waiting for the Huns that are bound to come again. And the rest of the time we live like moles, almost blindly in the mud. From dawn to dusk we see nothing but mud, and the strip of sky above us.

Old Fritz is always ready to pick off any man who shows his head, and he'll sometimes blast away at nothing at all with his rifles and machine guns. We learn rather quickly to listen for the shells from his big guns and judge—by the sound they make—whether we should duck our heads or get up and try to dodge them. Some days he fairly keeps us hopping.

But other days are rather peaceful. We spend hours talking about our families and our homes. Some of the lads are forever writing letters, and others play endless games of cards. There's always a little crowd that comes to watch me whittle.

Here's a pair of funny fellows, enclosed, to add to your

army. One is catching a bit of rest while he can. In a moment, someone will kick him awake and send him to work with a shovel. The other is a different sort. Every morning this chap brings up our breakfast in big tin pots. Others come with him to carry our mail, and they take away the letters that we've just written. It's the high point of the day, hot food and letters straight from England. Right now, the chap beside me is reading yesterday's Times!

It's a funny thing, but the war stops at breakfast. Fritz doesn't shoot at us, and we don't shoot at him. If the wind is right, we can even smell his bacon cooking. This morning I tried to pitch a biscuit to him. But I don't think it reached the wire.

> *All my love, forever,*
> *Dad*

I was disappointed by the first figure that I found inside the package, the man who brought the breakfast. It made me smile to see his arms stretched so long by the weight he carried that his hands reached nearly to his ankles. But I wanted soldiers, not messmen, and he would look rather silly, I thought, running over no-man's-land with kettles in his hands. I stood him on the table and took the wrappings from the second man.

"Oh, he's a darling," said Auntie Ivy.

He lay on his side, curled into a ball like a khaki-colored kitten. He had an old Burberry pulled over his shoulders, his forearm for a pillow. His cap was twisted sideways and his face smiling, as though his dreams were happy.

"I'll make him a dead man," I said.

"Oh, Johnny," said Auntie Ivy. "Do you have to think of things like that?"

"But I don't have any dead men," I told her.

"You should count yourself lucky." She turned her chair sideways and read my other letter, from my mum this time.

I always closed my eyes to hear my mother's letters. She wrote just the way she talked, and Auntie's voice was a lot like hers, so it seemed that Mum was there beside me.

"There is great pressure on all the men to do their bit and enlist. Today Mr. Brown joined Kitchener's army, and you know very well how little like a soldier he looks. But it must be nice to feel wanted by someone. I think that every man in London could be off to France and there still!! would be no work for women. If you're not a nurse or a seamstress there's precious little you can do, except stay home and knit wretched socks!"

Auntie Ivy *tsk*ed.

"I got a scare last night, when the guns started shooting in Regent's Park. I looked out and saw the searchlights sweeping across the sky. Back and forth they went, making circles on the clouds. The shells burst above them, with flashes like lightning. I didn't see a zeppelin. Maybe there wasn't even one there. But I thanked my lucky stars that you're safe and well looked after."

I took my new soldiers out to the garden, and stood the messman in the Tommies' trench. I put the other down in no-man's-land, then covered his foot with a bit of mud, to make it look as though he had been there for a long time. He made my battlefield look proper and gory.

I hurled some shells about, but didn't have time for a battle. The potting shed and the ground around it were littered with the remains of Mr. Tuttle's roses. I felt like a killer, with Scotland Yard closing in; I had to get rid of the evidence. I hid the branches deep in the forest. I carried away the leftover mulch and scattered it among the bushes. Then I built my bonfire with the bits that were left, disguising them below a layer of twigs and moldy leaves. It was the saddest little fire I'd ever seen, no bigger than a pudding.

As soon as darkness came, Auntie Ivy touched a match to the shreds of rotten leaves. They fizzled but wouldn't burn. They filled the garden with a thick smudge of smoke.

Auntie Ivy said "Ooooh!" as the Crimson Rain squirted up in a crackly spurt. She said "Gracious!" when my first whizz-bang sputtered and popped. Then the second one went off with a tiny yellow flame, and Auntie Ivy said, "Are you finished now? It's getting rather cold."

"I have to burn the guy," I said.

"Well, hurry up," she told me.

I dragged him from his corner, his poor head lolling on its strings. He was more than twice my size, but I heaved him up to my shoulders and staggered with him round my little fire.

"Guy, guy, guy," I sang. "Stick 'im in the eye."

"Watch your shoes," cried Auntie Ivy. "You'll scorch your good shoes."

I looked down and saw that the fire was right between my feet. It had dwindled already to ashes and embers.

"Get away from there," snapped Auntie.

I stepped back, and tripped over the guy's dangling leg. I fell in a heap on top of him, and the prickly thorns of Mr. Tuttle's roses stabbed me through the burlap body.

Auntie Ivy laughed. I heard her voice rising shrill and cackly, and I stared between my feet at my sick little fire, at the tattered pink remains of my precious whizz-bangs. Beyond them, over the black bulk of the stone wall, a fizz of sparks gleamed from a distant bonfire. A rocket shot up and exploded, and a flower of red light opened in the sky. A faint howl of voices came over the fields from Cliffe.

I thought of all the wonderful Guy Fawkes Days I'd spent in London, the shrieking and the laughter as a dozen boys danced our guys around fires so high that they towered above us. I remembered the heat and the roar of the flames. Far away, another rocket blossomed into orange.

"Auntie?" I said. "Can we go to Cliffe? Can I take my guy to the fire?"

"Certainly not," she said. "I'm not walking all the way to Cliffe to see a lot of hooligans."

"Please?" I said.

"You can go yourself," she told me.

I stamped out my little fire, the worst I'd ever seen,

and went off alone to Cliffe. I carried my guy for half a mile, dragged him a bit, then carried him again. The night was very black, and the fireworks flared in red and yellow and silver. Whizz-bangs exploded, and jumping-crackers rattled like gunshots, and I thought of myself trudging up to the front. The sound of the crackers, the faint smell of powder, made me think of my father, and how he'd seen the guns blazing in the distance.

I had left the farm behind me, and was passing the woods. In the flashes of the rockets I could see the bare branches of the trees tangled against the sky. Across my shoulders, the guy lay like a wounded man. And I carried him all the way to the village, to the old stone church at its center.

There the bonfire raged. Its flames soared up from an enormous pile of wood and branches, licking with yellow tongues at a great cloud of shimmering sparks. Around it ran the boys, their guys leaping and tumbling like gangly creatures that chased them through the heat and roar. The adults and the girls stood in a ring facing the fire, and the light made their cheeks a dazzling red, their eyes as black as voids. In their dark clothes, standing absolutely still, they looked a village of dead people, their faces only skulls.

"Guy, guy, guy," the boys chanted. "Stick 'im in the eye."

They circled the fire as embers exploded into bursts of sparks. The roar and the popping, the sharp cracks of whizz-bangs, made me think again of the war. The boys were like soldiers running through shell bursts.

"Guy, guy, guy. Stick 'im in the eye."

They shrieked and laughed. The fire raged.

"Hang him on a lamppost. And there let 'im die."

One by one, the guys went soaring up, flung by the boys to the top of the bonfire. Their stuffed legs seemed to kick at the wood and the flames. Their arms groped through the sparks, and their masked faces grinned as the fire swept over them. They sprawled on the wood and burst into fire themselves. Their bodies tore open, spilling out smoke. One came hurtling down, wrapped all in flames, rolling over and over as his arms beat at the fire in his burlap body. I dragged my own guy forward and heaved him up with the rest.

He seemed to sit for a moment at the very top, his huge head flopping forward. His arms seemed to lift and beckon to me, to all of us. Then the fire took hold of his ankles and crept up his legs. Smoke welled from the body, thick coils of gray that swirled around his monstrous head, around his tiny little cap. The boys laughed to see him, my poor sad guy. But I looked at him almost with horror as the clothes my father once had worn blackened and twisted, then burst into flames. The smoke thickened. My guy's body split open and Mr. Tuttle's rosebushes tumbled down into the heart of the bonfire. His head tipped back, and a split appeared for his mouth, holes for his eyes. They jetted smoke, then turned to fiery red from the blaze of twigs inside. He seemed to glare at me, to shout in the roar of the fire. Then his strings dissolved and he collapsed into pieces, and only his head was left, smoldering into ashes that drifted up with the sparks.

There was silence for a moment; then the boys all shrieked and hollered. They jostled against me, pushing me sideways. I stumbled back against one, who shoved me on to the next. The firelight swept over them, flickering on their clothes and faces. It made them strange and savagelike, and they laughed and chanted.

"Guy, guy, guy. Stick 'im in the eye."

They pushed harder. I reeled from boy to boy. Sparks burst from the fire, exploding at my feet.

"Hang him on a lamppost. And there let 'im die."

The ring of watching skulls gaped at me. The boys pushed me closer to the fire. What had started as a game, I thought, had turned to a wildness they couldn't control. Their hands pressed and shoved.

I felt the whole heat of the bonfire scorching at my back, and I feared the boys would throw me on it. They would pitch me up—I was certain they would—and my arms would flail like those of the guys as I fell, spread-eagled, on the wood.

Then Sarah was there, swirling in among the boys, and I thought she had come to pull me away. But when she took my hands she pushed me instead, and I spun around to find more hands waiting. I slipped into the rhythm then, into a mad sort of dance, a Red Indian dance of stamping feet and whoops and shouts. We flew round and round, under the sparks and the whirls of smoke, round and round the watching faces.

I was sad when it ended. The boys went off in pairs and little groups, and the great fire dwindled to a heap of coals. Soon Sarah and I were the only ones left, and we walked together to the edge of the village. I didn't mind her being there. Her hair had a particular smell that I liked very much, a lovely mix of smoke and gunpowder.

It wasn't so bad, I thought, to have a girl for a friend. After all, she was almost like a boy. Except for her clothes and her hair, and her voice and her shape, she was *exactly* the same as a boy.

CHAPTER 7

November 11, 1914

Dearest Johnny,

I can't tell you exactly where I am, as our commanding officer would not allow it. He is a very kind soul who is loath to read our letters at all. But he must, and he does.

The best I can say is that we're somewhere near a town called Ypres. Goodness knows how you're supposed to pronounce it. We call it Wipers.

We're not quite close enough that we can see the village, but I can tell where it is by the smoke that rises from the ruins. The Hun, unable to capture it, has decided to destroy it instead. He did the same thing in Belgium, of course, smashing the very best and oldest buildings like a child in a tantrum. Bit by bit, all the land around us, all the homes and the trees, are vanishing in the same way. Before very long there will be nothing but endless ruin and mud.

It's the dreariest world. And the dreariest weather. Bitterly cold, it only stops raining when it starts to snow or sleet instead. We are settling down for winter, the first British soldiers to ever do that in the field. War used to stop when the snow began falling. But now it just goes on.

*The shells come down, the bullets fly, at dawn and dusk
we stand to. We're still waiting for Fritz to come at our
throats, and sometimes I wish he would. I wish he'd come
and get it over with. The waiting is very hard for me.*

*Enclosed is a sniper. The fellow stands for hours, as still
as a heron in the marsh, watching through a tiny hole for a
glint of sun along the German parapet. I envy him, Johnny.
All that I ever see is mud, and a little bit of sky.*

        All my love, forever and ever,
        Dad

I was setting up the sniper when Sarah came by. She
arrived on the footpath, hopping over the wall by the
beech tree. "What are you doing?" she asked.

"There's going to be a battle." I pointed at my nutcracker men lined up in their trench. "The Huns are going to attack."

"They shouldn't do that," said Sarah.

"Why not?"

"Because they don't." She put her hands on her hips.
"That's what my dad says. They like to wait in the
trenches for the British to come, then shoot them down
with machine guns."

I didn't like being told by a girl how to fight my battles. "They can attack if I want," I said.

"You should have a raid instead," she told me. "Raids
happen all the time."

"I know," I said. "My dad says he's seen them."

"Well, *my* dad leads them," said Sarah. "He gets volunteers, and he takes them out into no-man's-land, right
across to the German trenches."

"And then what?" I asked.

"Different things." She acted them out with her hands. "Sometimes they throw bombs in the trench. Sometimes they go rushing in themselves, and they grab a German and haul him out." She cupped a hand to her ear. "Sometimes they just lie there and listen."

"All right." I showed her the little lieutenant with his long coat and his whistle. "This can be your dad," I said.

Sarah took it from me. I thought she would marvel at the perfect little man, but she only sniffed and curled her lip. "I suppose it will *do,*" she said. "He wouldn't *really* wear his trench coat on a raid, but that's all right."

"Make him ask for volunteers, and my dad will go." I picked up the whittled model of my father. "They can crawl across no-man's-land right here, and—"

"*You* can't make the orders," said Sarah. "*I'm* the officer, *you're* just the soldier."

We put our wooden men in their places. The lieutenant shouted, "I need volunteers!"

Up popped my little dad. "Me, sir!" he cried.

The lieutenant nodded, his whole body tipping. "Who else?"

"Just me," said my dad.

Sarah breathed hard through her nose. "Johnny, there *has* to be another one. You can't have a proper raid with just one soldier."

I chose the sergeant. "I suppose I'll go," he grumbled.

Sarah knelt by the trench. In her hand, the lieutenant squirmed over the top, onto the muddy slope of no-man's-land. "It's very dark," she said, in the gruff voice of the wooden lieutenant. "It's the middle of the night. So stay close behind me, and keep low to the ground."

My little man with his little rifle went out next, and then the sergeant. They squirmed across the mud.

"Get down!" said Sarah's lieutenant. She pressed him into the ground. "The Huns have fired a star shell, and I think they might have seen us."

She punched the ground. Mud splashed up through her knuckles. "Boom!" she shouted.

I pecked out machine-gun bullets. "Ratta-tatta-tat." My fist hurtled down like a shell. "Whizz . . . boom!" My dad started moving. He slithered past a twig, around a stone, and crept toward my dead man.

"Bang, bang, bang!" shouted Sarah. She hurled a handful of mud. "Boom!"

Bullets sprayed around my dad, around the dead man on the ground. The lieutenant got up and scuttled forward.

It was too hard to move both of my men and fire bullets at the same time. "The sergeant's scared," I shouted, and sent him scampering back to the trenches. "We'll have to go on by ourselves."

"Follow me!" cried the lieutenant.

Bullets whizzed around the little men. The ground heaved where I punched at the garden. But my father crept closer to the German trenches. "Ratta-tatta-tat!" He lay flat for a moment, then got up and dashed forward, leaping into the trench before the lieutenant could get there. He battled with my nutcracker men, and they toppled all around him. Then he grabbed the last one and scampered back.

General Cedric ran up from his place behind the lines. "Splendid work," he said. "You'll get a Victoria Cross for this, Private Briggs."

The wooden lieutenant crawled back through shell bursts and bullets, dragging the sleeping man—the dead man—behind him. "Wounded," he said. "The chap's only wounded."

I wished I had thought of that for myself. It made the lieutenant look brave and heroic.

"I got right to the trench," said Sarah, in the lieutenant's voice. He stood up again. "I heard the Germans talking, and they're going to start a barrage. Look how angry they are."

The evening sun slanted into the German trench, shining on my nutcracker men, gleaming on their teeth and their bayonets. They looked fiercer than ever.

We collected stones and balls of mud, heaping them against the wall. But General Cedric canceled the barrage, because Auntie called me in for tea.

That night, a Friday, she dragged her big tin basin into the kitchen, and I had a bath in front of the stove, behind a barricade of quilts and blankets. She found my grandfather's old dressing gown, and I sat bundled inside it as I wrote to Mum and Dad. It would become a ritual on Friday nights: a bath, a cup of Horlicks, letters to my parents.

I shivered through the chore that first time, turning out two letters exactly the same, except one started Dear Mum and the other Dear Dad. "I am fine. How are you?" I wrote. "Auntie Ivy is fine. Tomorrow I have to go and see Mr. Turtle." I crossed that out. "Mr. Tuttle."

His house was just a ten-minute walk down the road. On the outside, it was simple and thatched. But inside, it was full of things, of little plates and frilly doilies, of photographs and keepsakes. On a shelf was a picture in a black frame, the portrait of a lady with long hair coiled in tight little turns, as though a hundred watch springs had exploded from her dark-colored bonnet. "Is that your daughter?" I asked.

"No, Johnny." He took out a handkerchief and dusted the glass, though it already sparkled. "That was Mrs. Tuttle. Rest her soul."

The handkerchief dabbed at the frame, then at his eyes. But when he turned around, he was smiling. "We'd best get started with our lessons."

Two enormous chairs faced the fire, with a table between them where he'd set a copy of the *Iliad,* a plate of biscuits and two glasses of milk slicked with cream. The chair swallowed me up; it was soft as meringue. Mr. Tuttle picked up his book.

"This is a story about a war," he said. "A very old war. It was written nearly three thousand years ago, but you might think that Homer finished it just this morning. He comes so close to describing the events of today that it's uncanny, really."

He paced across the hearth, just as he paced in school. His hands went up to his collar, as though reaching for the gown that he always wore in class.

"Homer begins by talking about the gods in their palaces among the clouds. They're all related, by marriage and birth, and always bickering with each other. For amusement they toy with the people. To the gods, the people are merely pieces in a great game."

In class, Mr. Tuttle was strict and stern. But in his home he was different, not nearly so dull. "Now think of Kaiser Wilhelm, the leader of Germany. Queen Victoria was his grandmother, our King his cousin. As boys, the

Kaiser and the King fought imaginary battles in a toy fort not terribly far from here."

He paced past my chair. "Well, the Kaiser grew up, but he never stopped his games. He sported himself in fanciful uniforms that hid his crippled arm. He outdid his cousin with a better navy and a bigger army, an enormous army dressed in toy-soldier clothes. He and all the rulers of Europe are just like Homer's gods, all related, always fighting. Do you see that, Johnny?"

"Yes, sir," I said.

"I knew you would." He opened the book and turned through the pages. "So in the sky we have the gods, and down on the earth there's Agamemnon, the King of ancient Greece. He has been at war with the Trojans for nine years, all because of a silly argument between two princes, his own brother Menelaus and a Trojan named Paris. As the *Iliad* begins, the gods are toying with Agamemnon. They let him dream that he can capture the city of Troy and at last bring an end to this war. Agamemnon wakes up believing the gods will make him win. Understand?"

"Yes, sir." I nodded. "Like the Kaiser."

"Quite right. The Kaiser has always taught his men that God is on their side," said Mr. Tuttle, pacing. "Agamemnon marches against Troy. Guarding the city are the Trojans, led by Hector, the bravest of them all. He sees the Greeks swarming toward him, an army so huge that its men are like blades of grass in a field. Hector's army is tiny; he knows he cannot win. But does he surrender? No. Does he close the city gates?" Mr. Tuttle's eyes bulged as he stabbed a finger in the air. "No! He fights back nonetheless. Now who does that remind you of?"

"Belgium," I said.

"Good, Johnny. Yes, Belgium fought to a brave finish. But who else might fear the Kaiser coming?"

"France?" I said.

"Yes. But what about Britain? We're a tiny nation, our army dwarfed by Germany's."

"But we can't be Hector," I said.

"Why is that?"

"Because we have to win."

"Ah." Mr. Tuttle put his book on the table. "Isn't that what every Trojan would have thought?"

I had never once imagined that Britain might *lose* the war. "What happens next?" I asked.

Mr. Tuttle beamed. "The armies clash; they battle back and forth. Agamemnon fears the gods have deserted him, so he pulls his men away and shelters them in trenches."

"Like the Kaiser did," I said.

"Exactly like the Kaiser did."

I leaned forward. "And then what happens?"

"You tell me." Mr. Tuttle tapped on the cover of his *Iliad*. "You read this book and tell me then: what did all the men of both the armies pray for at the same time?"

"Victory?" I asked.

"Don't guess," he said. "Read the *Iliad,* Johnny. It's all in there."

He sat with me then, and we drank our milk and ate our cookies. He talked about other books in a way that wasn't too terribly boring. I was starting to think that I might escape the thing I'd been dreading when he asked for my help in his garden.

"It won't take long," he said. "A few minutes is all."

He led me through the house and out to the battered roses. He asked me to hold the bushes open while he wrapped the broken stems in bandages of tape and burlap. He was like a doctor tending to the wounded.

"The poor roses," he said. "I imagine that most of them ended up on that bonfire. Wouldn't you say that's likely?"

"It might be, sir," I said.

"I should have gone and watched the guys being burned." Mr. Tuttle lay nearly flat on the ground as he reached in among the roses. "I might have seen the branches tumble from one of them like a telltale heart."

He twisted his neck to look back at me. "But I couldn't bear to watch it, Johnny. I would have flown into a rage, I think."

I tried to smile. There was nothing to say.

"I've fought against blight, against drought and frost. I've battled dogs and birds and insects," he said. "I never thought that I'd be beaten by a boy."

"What will you do if you find him?" I asked.

"I don't have to find him at all." His face was turning red. "I already know the boy who did this."

My heart leapt to my throat. I let go of the branches, and they sprang shut like a spring-loaded trap, stabbing his skin with their thorns.

Mr. Tuttle let out a little gasp. "Open them, please," he whispered.

They popped and snapped at his sweater, unraveling strands of wool. Mr. Tuttle breathed a few wheezy breaths, then went back to his work.

"I know *all* the boys," he said. "So I'm bound to know

the vandal. I shall let it be known what was done to my roses, and I'm sure the boy will come to me. I believe his guilt will get the better of him."

"What will you do to him, sir?" I asked.

"The boy will spend a year with me. A full twelve months," said Mr. Tuttle. "Rain or shine, summer and winter, every day for a year he will come to my garden and tend to my roses."

"But what if he doesn't own up?"

"Then I'll lose all hope for the boys of Cliffe," he said. "I'm too old to struggle anymore. If no one has come forward by Christmas, I shall resign from the school."

He tucked his bandages round the broken stems, and his voice turned slow and sad. "I should miss the classroom," he said. "Apart from the garden, it's all I have. But nonetheless, my mind is made up. It's a matter of principles, Johnny."

I felt rotten inside. But I couldn't possibly admit to what I'd done if it meant staying for a year in Cliffe. I was going home when the war ended; I was going home at Christmas.

"Principles are taking men to the front," said Mr. Tuttle. "Principles sent Agamemnon marching against Troy. Without his principles a man has nothing; he *is* nothing. Even a dog, after all, has principles."

At last he turned me free. He squirmed out from under his bushes, and stood with the last tattered bandages dangling from his fist. He told me to go along home, and not to worry about his roses. "If they last the winter, they'll last forever," he said.

In my hurry to leave, I nearly gave myself away by slipping through the tunnel in his hedge. But I stopped in time, and circled around his wall to reach the footpaths that would take me home.

The sun was setting, the autumn days already short. Darkness settled in the hollows of the path, in the bushes along its sides. An owl hooted at me, then fluttered away like a shadow.

I passed the ruined cottage and came to the cemetery. The barren old trees bowed over the graves like mourners, their tops nodding in a breeze that came from the river, over the marshes. Behind them, on the farmhouse balcony, stood a figure all in black, veils and shawls fluttering in the wind that smelled of mud.

It was Mrs. Sims, in her mourning clothes, and she was looking down at the little graveyard between us. The mounds of leaves banked against the tombstones looked like freshly dug graves. In the shadows and the growing darkness, I thought I saw them moving.

I stood behind a scrag of bushes. Mrs. Sims turned on the balcony, leaning forward with her hands on the railing. It was me she was looking at, trying to pick me out among the branches and bushes.

Then I heard a slithering sound, and the leaves moved again. I gasped with a sudden fright, then laughed when a cat appeared among them, a white-and-orange tabby that stretched and shook itself.

I started walking again, and Mrs. Sims lifted her head. The black clothes swirled around her, and she looked like cold Mr. Death standing up there.

CHAPTER 8

November 18, 1914

Dearest Johnny,

I went over the top last night, and I'm quivering in my boots this morning to think what a narrow escape I had. A lieutenant chose your old dad and two other chaps to launch a little raid against the Hun, the sort of nuisance thing that keeps him on his toes. We smeared our faces with blacking and set off at midnight. Over the parapet we went, one by one, armed with wire cutters and little bombs.

It was the strangest feeling to come out of the trench and start across no-man's-land. What a sense of freedom and of horror! To leave all the lads behind and go alone through the mud—Johnny, I don't know how to tell you. To feel a breeze on my face for the first time in nearly a week—it was indescribably lovely. But the place was dreadful, and so utterly black that it filled me with fear. I think I knew how a bird must feel to leave the nest for the first time, to flutter through air that can't seem to hold him.

All the men that I'd glimpsed each day at dawn and at dusk, those poor souls who seemed to be sleeping, still lay exactly where they'd been when I first arrived at the front. I slithered past them, on toward the wire, and—it's strange to say—they seemed a bit like friends of mine. In their sightless eyes, I felt a comradeship with them. There they lay, with no purpose, it seemed, but to shelter me with their bodies.

A star shell burst. Its white light flared brighter than the sun, I thought. Not thirty yards away, there were Germans swinging their machine guns from shadow to shadow, just waiting to see a movement. I pressed myself down behind one of those sleeping men.

Well, something must have drawn the Germans' attention, for a gun swung toward me. I heard the sound of it, that awful mechanical chatter. Then the mud started to bubble close at my side. A second gun found me, and a third. They crossed to meet me like spotlights on an actor. And I did my best—believe me—to act very still.

I pressed myself against that sleeping man. I had my hand on his ankle, my head on his thigh. And I saw his uniform—or the tatters of it—and knew the man was German. In life, he'd done his best to kill me. But now, in death, he hid me and he sheltered me. I don't know if you'll understand this, but I felt a kinship with him, Johnny. It seemed to me, hunkered down there—frozen with fright— that he had gone beyond the battle, somehow. That he was content to lie there in a land that belonged to no man, and offer protection to anyone who needed it.

The flare fizzled out. But another burst behind it. The Germans kept shooting, and our own guns opened up, the bullets whistling past above my head. But the sleeping man kept me safe, until the darkness came and I carried on. I rolled away from him and wormed my way toward the wire.

We reached the German trench that night. We bombed it, and even brought back a Hun for a prisoner. There was *an extra tot of rum for all of us when we dragged him in from no-man's-land.*

This morning, when I stood at the parapet, I looked for my sleeping friend. And the funny thing is that he wasn't there. It's possible that the bullets shifted him about, or the ground collapsed around him. But I like to think that he had done his job and moved along. To where, I can't imagine.

You will find, enclosed, a new soldier for your army. I'm sorry, but I didn't have time to paint him.

> *All my love,*
> *Dad*

Of all the letters that Dad had sent, this one was my favorite. I listened to it smiling, my eyes open but seeing my own little battlefield, my trench full of nutcracker men. I felt as though I was fighting the battle side by side with my dad, that we were going together across no-man's-land. His raid was so close to the one that I had imagined that the letter might have been sent by my wooden soldier.

"Well, open your parcel," said Auntie Ivy.

I had almost forgotten that I held a new man in his wrappings. "It was just like that in the garden," I said.

"Like what?" she asked.

"The raid." I tore the paper. "I was playing with Sarah, and we had a raid just like that, just like Dad's."

"I'm sure it's *all* the same," she said. "Your trenches, your bombs."

The package fell open and the soldier slid out.

"Oh, my," said Auntie. "I don't care for that."

The figure crawled on all fours, one hand reaching

forward, one leg dragging behind. Carved from pale wood, unpainted, he seemed utterly weary, as though he could hardly move another inch. But there was a feeling of strength in him too, so I could look at him and *know* he'd keep going.

"Oh, my," said Auntie again.

Then I saw what shocked her. It was the soldier's face. Below his carved hat, there *was* no face. Instead, the soldier had the broad and flattened muzzle of a bulldog.

"Poor James," said Auntie. "Oh, your poor father. What did he see out there in the trenches?"

The little dog-faced soldier wasn't ugly. He looked rather brave to me. "I think he's going forward against the Huns," I said. "I think he's going to carry on no matter what goes wrong."

"Well, I don't want to look at him," she said.

I picked up the figure. "I'll put him in the line."

"Just take it away." She shook her hands, as though it was a spider that I held. "Just take it away."

"Yes, Auntie."

I went out the back and found Sarah waiting by the wall. I ran toward her. "A raid!" I cried. "My dad went over the top; he went out on a raid."

"Well, didn't I tell you?" she said. "*My* dad's been on a dozen raids, on twenty raids, maybe. They always have raids."

"It was just the same," I said. But she didn't care.

Below the beech tree, she had started a second pile of muddy ammunition. "Johnny, let's have our barrage," she said.

I placed my new soldier in the line. He didn't look right hunched in the bottom of the trench, so I moved him forward until he was crawling up the parapet. His strange, animal face peered over the edge, and I ducked down to see what he would see.

My no-man's-land looked enormous then, sloping up toward the German lines. My nutcracker men were hidden, but the tips of their silver bayonets poked up from the mud like the pickets of a ragged fence. I wished I could make myself tiny and go charging toward them.

"Johnny, come on," said Sarah.

I stood beside her near the tree, the pile of stones and mud between us. We filled our hands with shells.

"You fire the big guns," said Sarah. "I'll be the mortars and the Moaning Minnies."

I didn't even know what those were. But as soon as Sarah started shooting, I wished that *I* had the Moaning Minnies.

These guns fired whole handfuls of dirt and pebbles, with a bloodcurdling shriek that reminded me of the sounds I'd heard from the farmhouse. "Shhreeeeee!" Sarah yelled, and threw the dirt. "Bam! Bam-bam!"

I took the biggest clumps of mud and tossed them high in the air. "Whizz. Bang!" They exploded behind the British trenches, sending bits of shrapnel skittering over the ground.

"Blast those Tommies!" shouted Sarah in a German accent. "God punish England!" Her mortars popped and boomed, her Moaning Minnies sent lumps of mud screaming past me. She bent down, grabbed more dirt and threw more bombs. *"Aarrgh!"* cried the Tommies. And the Germans said, "Again! Punish them again."

My big guns kept firing, slowly and methodically. I

hurled the stones—"Whizzz!"—tossed up my hands—
"Bang!"

We rained the Tommies with dirt and stones. We
worked our way through our pile of ammunition, until
only the largest shells were left. Then Sarah, too, started
firing the big guns. She bobbed down, popped up again,
hurling the stones like a shot-putter. Then she hit the
British trench. And she crushed the first Pierre.

"Don't!" I shouted.

I threw myself down by the trench and rolled the
stone aside. Frantically, I scrabbled through the mud. I
dug and dug, but all I found were the Frenchman's feet.
The rest of him was gone.

"Look what you did!" I cried. "You broke him, you
clot." I clawed at the mud, searching for Pierre's body.
"My dad made that for me and you've gone and broken
him, you clumsy oaf."

"I'm sorry, Johnny." Sarah panted. Her face was red,
her hair in tangles. "I didn't mean to do it."

I was digging like a dog. "At least help me look,"
I said.

"Not if you're going to talk like that." She stomped
away. "I'm not going to help someone who shouts," she
said, and climbed the wall and left me there.

I kept searching for the rest of my Frenchman. I
looked until supper, and again until dark, but he seemed
to have vanished, as though the shell had blown him into
smithereens. I hated Sarah then; I would never play with
her again, I said.

At school I avoided her. When classes ended I dashed
home on the footpaths to play by myself in the garden. I

cleaned up the rubble and rock, then scraped out my trenches where the barrage had caved them in. I shifted my Tommies out of the way, standing them up on the mud above the trenches. But the metal soldiers couldn't balance on the broken ground, and they toppled over on their sides and their backs. I said that snipers had got them. "Watch out, lads," I said.

Nearly the entire front line was in order when I heard footsteps coming up to the wall. "You can't come in here," I said, thinking it was Sarah. "Go home."

But a man's voice answered. "I have nowhere to go."

I looked up from the trenches. Behind the wall stood a sergeant, his legs and waist hidden behind it, his elbows on the stone. In his teeth was a pipe that wasn't lit, and his cap was pushed so far to the back of his head that it seemed it might fall off.

"What's your name?" I asked.

He took the pipe from his mouth. "What's yours? You tell me first."

"Johnny Briggs," I said.

"Ah. James must be your father." The sergeant stiffened, glancing up at the house. "He's not here, is he?"

"No," I said. "He's in France."

"Oh. Poor James."

"Do you know him?" I asked.

"I used to. When I was a boy I played in this garden." He pointed at me with his pipe. "Right where you are. I played there with James."

"Did he have his little gun?" I asked.

"Why, so he did." The sergeant stroked his cheeks. They were covered with thin white hairs that made his skin look oily. "Yes, I'd forgotten that, his little gun."

"That's him," I said, pointing down at my trenches, at the figure my dad had made.

"That wooden-headed chap? Yes, that would be James."

"He's holding his little gun," I said.

"He was never without it," said the sergeant. "He used to lie there, or kneel there, and tell me to come over the wall."

"Why?"

"So he could pick me off." The sergeant chuckled. "He was the British and I was the Boer. Sometimes I was a Zulu, not that it mattered in the end. I always came over the wall screaming like a lunatic, and he always picked me off."

It made me giggle, the thought of my father being a boy.

"Where is he, in France?" the sergeant asked.

"Well, look," I said, pointing again. "In the trenches, see? Right at the front."

"It's a very long front," said the sergeant. "In parts of it, there's no fighting at all. The Germans stay in their trenches, and the British stay in ours, and between them there's grass and trees, there's rabbits and birds. But in other places . . ." His eyes darkened. "They go at it tooth and claw. Go at it night and day, across a waste of slime and mud. You sleep with your rifle in your hands, your bayonet fixed. You hurl your shells at Fritz, and he hurls his shells at you, and the noise can drive you mad."

"*That's* where my dad is," I said.

"Then 'poor James' he is," said the sergeant.

"Is that where you were?"

"Somewhere like that."

"Are you going back?"

He shook his head.

"Why not?"

"I fought, I lost, and that's the end of it," he said.

"Why did you lose?"

"Because they beat us."

"Won't the army make you go back?"

"I don't see how they can." He tapped his pipe on the wall, then slipped it into his pocket. "Even the worst of butchers runs his meat only once through a mincer."

He lifted his hand again, and there was something else in it. He pitched it over the wall, into the garden, and I scrambled to fetch it as it tumbled over the mud.

I scooped it up from the trench. "Oh, golly!" I said. It was a brass cartridge, a bullet casing.

I turned to thank the sergeant, but he was gone. Even when I stood up I couldn't see him, as though he had vanished into the forest.

I held the cartridge up to my lips and blew across the opening. It made a lovely high whistle that echoed back from the house and the wall, from the trees of the forests and orchards. It filled all of Kent with a wonderful tingle, the same sound as a lieutenant's tin whistle, the sound that would send soldiers over the top.

Chapter 9

November 25, 1914

Dearest Johnny,

There is a great lot of fighting to the north of us. We can hear the shelling, and feel the blasts of the big Jack Johnsons. When the wind is right we smell the smoke and powder. The night sky sparkles with gun bursts.

On our right, the French took a pounding. Yet here the old hands say it's quiet. (Personally, I think they must be deaf! There's not an hour when a Moaning Minnie doesn't shriek overhead, or a bullet whistle past.) But the word is that the fighting will soon spread to our sector.

The other night, just after sunset, we heard Fritz marching. Thousands of boots marked thousands of steps along the duckboards of his trenches. It was a sound more terrible than the shells or the bullets, and it lasted all night long. At dawn we stood to, sure that the Boche would come up with the sun, pouring over no-man's-land like a river of gray.

But he didn't come then, and he didn't come this morning. Our only company are the rats and the lice. Frankly, I'd rather have those than Huns.

Sooner or later, though, they're bound to come. And the waiting is very hard. It's driving some men nearly mad. You can see it in their eyes, the strain of always waiting—for the next bullet, the next shell, the battle still ahead. They clean their rifles over and over, and volunteer for any duty at all from digging latrines to raiding trenches.

I'm glad I can sit here and whittle. I've spent the entire night, when I should have been sleeping, making an ambulance that you will find enclosed. You might find it rather familiar, son. At least I've solved the mystery of where all the buses have gone from London. Your little men will have to ride on top, but I don't suppose they'll mind.

Well, it's raining now, but it might change to snow very soon. I hope it does. I'd put up with a blizzard if it meant an end to this terrible mud.

Another shell just exploded on my right. A rush of men are going by with shovels and picks. A great deal of the trench gave way, but no surprises this time. The most astonishing things sometimes turn up when the parapet collapses.

I miss you dreadfully and wish I was there.
    All my love,
    Dad

Auntie Ivy folded the letter. She saved all of them in a little wooden box that she kept on a shelf above the stove, between her tea and her peppermint drops. She took her chair from the table and carried it there.

"Do you think Dad knew my Pierre got hurt?" I asked.

"How could he?" she said.

"Then why do you think he sent an ambulance?"

She stepped up on the seat. "I imagine he thought you might like it."

I tore the package open, and I smiled at first; the ambulance was beautiful. On its sides, Dad had painted the advertisements it would have carried as a bus. He'd put seats on the open roof, then smeared it all with mud and smoke.

But when I turned it over, I saw that one of the wheels was oddly twisted and smaller than the others. I blinked at it, suddenly sad. For the first time ever, my dad had made a toy that wasn't perfect, and I was glad that Auntie Ivy hadn't asked to see it.

"You'll be visiting Mr. Tuttle tonight," she said, taking the box from the shelf. She put the new letter inside. "Why don't you ask him to come and see your soldiers?"

"I'm not sure he'd want to," I said.

"Would it hurt you to ask?"

"No, Auntie." I took the ambulance out to the garden. I put it down in the mud, behind the British lines, and drove it toward the wall. It tilted over the ground, up and down through the shell craters that Sarah and I had made with our stones. I wondered if the bus conductor would still be standing at the door.

The ambulance stopped at the trench. "Any wounded?" the conductor shouted. "All wounded aboard." Then he pressed his little bell—"Ding, ding!"—and the driver started up.

I heard a laugh, and Sarah was there at the wall. "That's silly," she said. "They don't do it like that."

"They might," I said.

"They *carry* the wounded," she said. "How can you

climb on a bus if your arms are shot away? How can you walk if you haven't any legs?"

"Maybe they were only a little bit wounded," I said.

"You're *funny*, Johnny." She shook her head, just like my mum might have done. "No one's a *little* bit wounded. When the shells explode it's like the air's full of razors. Just the sound can kill you, if it's close enough. My dad says he's seen people blasted into so many pieces that he had to pick up the bits with a dustpan."

"Stop it," I said. I didn't want to hear about that.

"You can even die from a scratch," she said. "If a rat bites you, it might—"

"Stop!" I shouted. "I told you not to come here."

"I brought you something."

I still hated her, but I didn't mind looking at her present. I parked the ambulance and stood up.

Like the sergeant, she kept her hand behind the wall. "It's a present," she said. "Because I'm sorry your soldier broke. It's an aeroplane, Johnny."

She lifted her arm, the aeroplane zooming up as high as she could reach. It banked and swooped down, did a loop-the-loop in her hand, then landed on the wall. "It's yours to keep," she said.

It was hardly more than a block of wood, the sort of thing my dad would have mocked as "utter rubbish" and wouldn't have been caught dead even selling in his shop. I couldn't tell what type it was, or even which side it was on. But it was better than no aeroplane at all, and I said, "You can bring it into the garden."

She clambered over the wall and stood straddling the German trench, towering like a giant above my nut-cracker men. The aeroplane swooped in her hand, straight at the soldiers, then twisted along right on top of the trench.

"It wouldn't do that," I said, pleased to know more about something than Sarah. "It should stay up high. It's on reconnaissance."

"Why?"

"Because the Germans are going to attack." I looked her straight in the eye. "I don't care what you say. They're going to attack. You be the British, and you have to fight them off."

"If that's what you want," she said. "I suppose it *might* happen sometimes."

As we changed positions, the aeroplane became a German. It flew lazily over the battlefield until my nutcracker men were lined up and ready. Then I took out my brass cartridge and whistled. "Over the top!"

"I thought they were Germans," said Sarah.

"Over ze top!" I screamed, and whistled again.

Up swarmed the nutcracker men. They rose in a flood from the trench, pouring onto no-man's-land like the river of gray that my father had written about. They charged across in a rippling line as I pushed them along, two and three at once.

"Start shooting," I said. "You have to fight them off."

The aeroplane landed. Sarah took a metal machine gunner and swiveled him back and forth. "Boppa-boppa-boppa."

Six of the nutcracker men fell flat in the mud. The rest kept going. Already they were halfway to the British trenches.

"Where's the barbed wire?" asked Sarah. "They're supposed to tangle up in the wire."

"Just pretend they've passed it." I didn't have any barbed wire. "Keep shooting, Sarah."

"Boppa-boppa-boppa." A dozen more men fell in a row. *"Arrrgh!"* they shouted.

My hand was on Fatty Dienst. "Fight on for Chermany."

"Boppa-boppa-boppa."

The nutcracker men were coming up to the British trench. I told Sarah, "You'd better fix bayonets."

"Fix bayonets!" she shouted.

My whole German army balanced on the edge of the British parapet. I stepped across them to help the British. The messman ran up with his pots; the sleeping man woke and leapt to his feet. Little Cedric, far behind, said, "Send me reports. Tell me what's happening."

"The Huns are here!" shouted Sarah. She picked up the tiny lieutenant and charged him up to no-man's-land. He battled there, hand to hand against the nutcracker men.

"Ratta-tatta-tat." I worked the machine gunners, slamming the Germans down. Then I saw my wooden dad toppled in the trench. He got up and fired his rifle, and Fatty Dienst—the last German standing—crumpled into the mud.

"Oooh," said Sarah, panting. We grinned at each other, and I was sure she felt just as I did, that we'd fought a battle as real as real could be. My no-man's-land was covered with bodies, the earth torn up by the bullets. Like a pair of old soldiers, we talked about the battle as we gathered the dead and stood them back in their places.

"It gave me chills when you whistled them over the top," said Sarah. "That was so true."

I smiled, too proud to speak.

"Can I see your whistle?"

She was disappointed as soon as she touched the cartridge. "It's just a bullet," she said.

"It's not a bullet. It's a casing," I told her. "And it came straight from France."

"Then how did you get it?"

"From a soldier," I said. "I don't know his name."

Sarah tried to whistle with the cartridge. But the only sound she made was a fizz of air.

"Blow across it," I said. "Not right into it."

She tried again, then passed it to me, and I wiped off her spit and blew that wonderful shrill. Sharp and clear as the cry of a bird, it tingled right through me.

"Over the top!" shouted Sarah. "Johnny, let's fight them again."

We had another battle that was even bigger than the first one. The nutcracker men stormed over no-man's-land. One fell, and then another, but nothing would stop them. They came right to the trench, right over the parapet, spilling down in a shouting mass.

But the British trench was nearly empty. Only my dad and the little lieutenant were there to fight them off. Back to back, the wooden men battled with the Huns. Then General Cedric shouted, "Counterattack!" And I whistled, and the Tommies charged.

They leapt from the rear trench. The messman, the drill sergeant, all the lead soldiers, went bounding over the mud.

"*Gott in Himmel!*" cried the Germans as the machine guns opened fire.

"Ratta-tatta." "Boppa-boppa-boppa." Sarah's sounds

mingled with mine, as though guns of all sizes were shooting. The nutcracker men fell in great swaths, and the ones that were left went fleeing across no-man's-land.

"Ratta-tatta-tatta." Bullets pecked the mud at their feet.

"After them!" shouted Sarah. The lieutenant jumped up. Always the hero, he went like a fiend after the Huns.

I took the model of my dad and hopped him up onto no-man's-land. I shouted a battle cry and started to run him forward. But he got only a few feet before I stopped.

He was changing. He looked old and pale, not right at all. I lifted him up from the battlefield, a thousand feet up in his scale of little men. I cradled him in my hands.

"What's wrong?" asked Sarah.

"He's sort of broken," I said.

"Well, *I* didn't break him," said Sarah. "Don't say that *I* broke your man."

I didn't say anything. My lip was pinched in my teeth.

All my nutcracker men, all my Tommies and Frenchmen, looked as bright as they had on the day they were made. But the model of my father was changing. The khaki paint of his clothes had dulled to a moldy green. It had washed away from his knees and his arms, and was fading everywhere else. I could see the grain of the wood through his tunic and his trousers, the black swirl of a knothole starting to show in his chest. His mouth had once stretched in such a broad grin, but now it was small and grimly straight. A thin little crack—just as thick as a hair—had opened down his middle.

"Are you going to keep playing?" asked Sarah.

She was still on her knees in no-man's-land. The lieutenant stood by her, facing the nutcracker men, who seemed frozen in their mad rush toward safety.

"Johnny, are we going to finish the battle or not?"

I didn't care about that, or anything else. I felt as though I was looking at my real father, as though I was seeing him old and sick.

"Johnny!" Sarah stamped her feet. Mud sprayed from her shoes, and the wooden soldiers trembled. "Answer me!" she said.

I shook my head.

"Then I'm going home. And I'm taking my aeroplane with me."

She snatched it up and stomped across my no-man's-land. Her feet were like big Jack Johnsons, shaking the earth, flinging up dollops of mud. Specks of black shrapnel smacked against the nutcracker men, against the little lieutenant. The wooden soldiers stumbled and fell. The lieutenant cartwheeled into a crater. But Sarah kept walking, and she didn't look back.

Chapter 10

Dearest Johnny,

Just a short note this time, as I'm rather tired from all the events of the last few days.

Yesterday, late at night, we were taken out of the line and moved to the rear for a bit of a rest. The Huns were shelling us, of course, though not too heavily. We kept our heads down and moved along smartly, except when an incoming shell sounded particularly close and we flattened ourselves against the walls or the ground.

The fellow ahead of me was a blacksmith once. His name, oddly enough, was Harry Black, and he was my very best friend. We spent the last three days side by side, as close as newborn puppies. At breakfast yesterday he gave me half his plum-and-apple jam, and I let him share a little cake that your mother so kindly sent me. We planned to go for a very long walk tomorrow, until we learned that our officers had already lined up some amusements. Our period of rest, we learned, would be spent repairing a mile of shelled-out road and digging all sorts of new trenches.

About a week ago, before I really knew him, Harry

Black made a forage into no-man's-land one night and returned with one of those pickle-topped helmets that are worn by the Prussians, the type that is standard for your nutcracker army. He was the envy of us all when he put it on last night to make the trek to the rear, looking proud as Punch with his shiny new trophy. The mud that was tossed up by the shells rained on us all. But it rattled on Harry's head like pebbles in a tin cup, and he grinned at the rest of us, who could only cradle our arms across our cloth caps.

There's one spot on the way where the communication trench meets a stream. We have to rise to ground level, dash across the stream, then descend again into the earth. The sappers have built breastworks there, but old Fritz likes to watch that particular spot through the sight of his telescopic rifle. We call it Charing Cross, like the underground station, as it's surely the quickest route to the hospital.

Harry Black was nipping across when the Huns fired off a star shell. It fizzled right above us, making those ghastly shadows that they always do. Harry froze, but old Fritz must have seen the sparkle of light on his pickle-top helmet, for a bullet whizzed past me, and poor old Harry slumped to the ground. It was awful luck that the sniper missed his helmet and got him in the throat.

But I am fine and, as I say, enjoying my change if not my rest. I wouldn't pretend it's quite like Brighton Beach here behind the lines, but let me tell you that it was grand to sit and watch the sun go down. I'm only sorry that Harry couldn't see it. This morning he died of his wound.

He was such a good fellow that I've decided to enlist him for your army. You will find him, enclosed, just as I remember him.

Well, my little note has become a book. I'm so tired that I can hardly keep my eyes open.
All my love,
Dad

Neither Auntie nor I spoke for a long time. She stared at the letter, and I stared at her, hoping she would suddenly laugh and say there'd been a mistake, that the letter had been written by some other Dad, to some poor Johnny other than me. It wasn't at all like the letters he'd written before; it was hopeless and sad, as though he wasn't sure himself whether he should laugh or cry because his friend had been killed.

But Auntie didn't laugh. She put the letter down very slowly, and just as slowly picked up the one my mum had sent. "Are you going to open your parcel?" she asked.

It sat exactly between us, battered by the post, its paper stuffing spilling out through a slit. I knew what was in there: Harry Black, once my father's friend but now a dead man.

"Would you read Mum's letter first?" I asked.

She nodded. " 'Dear Johnny,' it says. 'The war touches us all.' " Her eyes kept straying to the parcel, and her voice, stopping and starting again, made my mum sound frightened too.

" 'Kindly Mrs. Vincent is now a widow, her sons—your chums—left fatherless. My heart goes out to them all. I heard the terrible news yesterday, and it was the last straw for me. I closed up our flat and took the train to Woolwich, back to my old position at the arsenal. Almost nothing has changed here since the day I left so many years ago. I felt sick at heart to see the pall of smoke and hear the din of machines. In the factory the people are still bending over their endless rows of shells. The only difference is that there are so many more of them now, shells and workers both.

" 'My job will be stuffing artillery shells. My hands can reach right down in the casings. It means I'll be working all day with sulphur and cordite, which is not the best thing to do. But at least I'm helping the war, and doing what I can to get the dreadful thing finished as soon as possible. I can hardly wait until the day that the three of us are together again, you and me and your dear, sweet father.' "

Auntie Ivy got up and put the letters in the box. She wobbled on the chair as she reached for the shelf, looking older than ever just then. "Now open your present," she told me.

I did it quickly, holding the parcel no nearer than my arms could stretch. I widened the slit with my fingers, reached through the wrapping, and pulled out the man by his head.

As soon as I saw Harry Black I knew why Dad liked him so much. The little man looked as jolly as anything. His legs were spindly but his chest enormous, his head dwarfed by a shining black helmet. He was doing a dance on one foot, his arms spreading out, one high and one low. The helmet covered his face, but I was sure that underneath it he was smiling.

Right away I felt happier. I danced like Harry danced, spinning across the kitchen floor. I danced down the hall and across the garden. I put the man down in my communication trench.

Suddenly, he didn't seem to be dancing. He looked out of balance, his arms and legs flung up to catch himself. He seemed to be falling.

I told myself not to think like that. The man was only dancing, I told myself. I said it aloud. "He's *dancing*, not dying."

I didn't really play with the soldiers. I moved them about, putting my father to work digging a trench. It pleased me to see that his paint hadn't faded any more, that the crack in his body wasn't getting any bigger. It was a silly thought, but I hoped that he might brighten again when my real dad felt rested and healthy.

Every day that week I went straight to the garden after school. I hurried home to see if the wooden model was brightening, but it wasn't. Then I sat and talked to the little man, pretending he was my real dad. I told him about Cliffe and about the boys, and how I was starting to be friends with some of them. I didn't tell him about Mr. Tuttle because I thought it might make him jealous. I talked in a whisper, looking only at my dad, trying not to see the dancing man. I was troubled by that figure, by the thought of what his face was really like below the big spiked helmet. I couldn't decide if it was happy, as I'd thought at first, or twisted into shock and pain. When Saturday came, I took the man with me. I didn't want him in the garden anymore.

Mr. Tuttle always smiled when he opened his door. But this time he looked down as I held the dancing man toward him, and his smile changed to a puzzled look. "You brought a toy," he said.

I blushed. "I brought it for you."

"You did?"

I nodded. "Yes, sir. I thought you might like it."

"Thank you," he said. "Johnny, thank you so much." He took the man from my fingers. "Why, it's magnificent."

"My father made it," I said.

"Did he? At the front?" Mr. Tuttle let the figure stand on his palm, in his fingers. He studied poor Harry Black from every angle. "It's—it's beyond words," he muttered. "It tells a whole story, doesn't it?"

"What story?" I asked, desperate to know if he would think the man was dancing or dying.

"It scarcely needs saying. He's one of the fallen," said Mr. Tuttle.

I shivered inside. "I thought at first he was dancing."

"Hardly," said Mr. Tuttle. "He was caught in the moment of death; anyone could see that. I don't know how, but your father's given a soul to this wooden soldier." He closed his fingers round the man and lifted it up to his face. "I can smell the mud on him, Johnny."

"Well, I put him in the garden," I admitted.

"The figurative mud," said Mr. Tuttle. "The corned beef, the cordite. The rigors of war. Tell me: has your father made any others?"

"Yes, sir," I said. "Lots."

"Do you think I might see them?" he asked.

"Oh, yes," I said. "I was going to ask you to come."

Mr. Tuttle was very pleased. He put Harry Black on his mantelpiece, among his Pickwick jugs and his statuettes. He didn't stand him upright, but set him on his side, and the little blacksmith suddenly looked more comfortable. Mr. Tuttle sighed. " 'There lies a dead man, unwept...' "

I recognized the quote and finished it for him. " 'Unburied.' "

Mr. Tuttle's eyebrows arched. "Johnny, you surprise me at every turn. You must be reading the *Iliad*."

"I'm nearly finished," I said. "It's rather good."

"Rather good?" he said loudly. "It's *brilliant*. It's wonderful."

We sat down and started our lesson. He picked up the story as the great armies of the Trojans and the Greeks were entrenched on the plains.

"They have clashed again and again," he said. "They have each taken terrible beatings. And now, in the tenth year of this war, the soldiers of both sides—the Greeks and Trojans alike—pray for the same thing. For what?"

"Peace," I said.

"Good, Johnny. And what happens? What miracle occurs?"

"A truce," I said.

"What sort of truce?"

"They agree to stop fighting if one man from each army comes out to fight a duel. And whoever wins will win the war."

Mr. Tuttle nodded. "And who fights this duel?"

"The men who started the war," I said.

"Yes!" cried Mr. Tuttle. He joggled the table in his excitement, sending biscuits flying. "Paris and Menelaus. The very two princes whose petty quarrel started all these years of war now walk out to settle it. They toss spears at each other. They go at it hand to hand. Then one of them captures the other, and the war is over, isn't it?"

"No," I said.

"Why not?"

"I think the gods start it up again," I said.

"Those meddling gods," said Mr. Tuttle. "The soldiers are homesick, scared and hungry. They want nothing else but the chance to go home. Yet the gods won't let them; they see to it that the fellow escapes, and they stir up the armies like hives of bees. Suddenly the war's back on, more savage than ever."

He took a biscuit, and his eyes jiggled as he chewed. "So," he said. "What do you think would happen in France if the British soldiers and the German soldiers agreed to end the war?"

"I don't know," I said.

"Well, think." He dribbled crumbs onto his lap. "If the Germans got so sick of fighting one day that they shouted across to your father—'Hello, there! Let's have a truce!'—what do you think would happen?"

"He would tell them where to get off," I said.

Mr. Tuttle smiled. "Would he? There he is, living in mud, worried about the bombs and the bullets, battling the rats and the lice and thinking always of you, and someone is telling him that he can go home if he wants. Don't you think he'd do that?"

"I'm not sure," I said.

"Well, I think he would," said Mr. Tuttle. "I think every soldier would. On both sides, to a man, they would put down their guns and go home."

"But they wouldn't be allowed to," I said.

"Who would stop them?"

"The Kaiser. The King."

"Ahh," said Mr. Tuttle. "The gods would intervene." He stood up, shedding the crumbs from his clothes. "You're quite right, Johnny. The Kaiser would never allow it. He loves his game of war, his men in their toy-soldier clothes."

"Maybe the King and the Kaiser will fight it out in no-man's-land," I said, and smiled to show I didn't really mean it.

"The King would give him a thrashing," said Mr. Tuttle.

I laughed, and that pleased him very much.

"But you've come to the heart of it, Johnny. What Homer is saying is that all the world is a game for the gods. Whatever you do, whether you're sitting here now or playing with your soldiers, it's because the gods want you to do it. But in the end they'll trick you, for you can never win if you fight against gods."

When our lesson ended that day I didn't feel in any hurry to go home. I sat in Mr. Tuttle's chair and told him how my dad was digging trenches for a rest, and how my mum had moved to Woolwich. Then *he* told *me* things about himself: that he'd taught in Cambridge at Trinity College and married a professor's daughter; that they'd moved to Cliffe because the weather suited roses; that the coming winter would be his seventh in the village. I became very fond of him that day. When it started to rain, first in drops and then in buckets, he grew worried for me.

"I wish you could stay," he said. "But you'd better be on your way before this gets any worse." He found an umbrella in his cupboard, and insisted that I take it.

The rain pelted down on the road, filling the ditches. It hammered on the umbrella until I could barely hold it upright. I felt like a Trojan being pelted by arrows, my shield above my head. I marched along through enormous puddles, the black clouds swirling close to the ground, stroking the trees with watery fingers.

I went straight to my garden. My little dad, paler than ever, lay up to his waist in water. I built a dugout that would keep him dry, then went to work on my trenches. The nutcracker men, on higher ground, were out of the rain, protected by the beech tree. But my British trenches were crumbling, so full of water that the wooden soldiers swam and the metal ones were close to drowning. Crouched under Mr. Tuttle's umbrella, I put it all in order. I dug channels to drain the trenches, then scraped away the ooze of mud that the water left behind.

I uncovered tiny snails and short, pink worms that wriggled in my fingers. And halfway down the line, I unearthed poor Pierre One, or the top half of him at least. His little wooden head jutted out from the wall of the trench, and I thought at first it was a snail's shell. But when I pulled him out, the mud tried to hold him in place. And he came free with a squelch and a pop: his head and arms, his shattered waist where Sarah's stone had snapped him into two. A worm wriggled away in the back of the hole, as though it had eaten the little man's legs.

I popped him on top of the ambulance, and the medic said, "I think he's a goner." But I gave him a ride to the back, tipped him off, and pretended that doctors were fussing over him. "Where's his legs?" they asked. "If we had his legs we could patch him up."

I couldn't remember where I'd put his legs. So the doctors said, "Died of his wounds. There's nothing we can do," and I buried him there at the back. I stood up a white pebble for his gravestone, and the doctors said, "He was a good soldier. He was a brave lad."

CHAPTER 11

December 8, 1914

Dearest Johnny,

My bit of rest ended quickly last night.

We were rushed back to the line very early this morning, well before daybreak and too suddenly to take anything but our rifles and our ammunition. We raced through the communication trench as the guns opened up. There was such an urgency and a haste that some of the lads went right over the open ground. I saw them above me, black shadowy men lit by the gun bursts.

At the front, all the soldiers were already standing to, though it wasn't yet dawn. We joined them, our rifles held up to the parapet, our faces pressed to the mud.

At the first crack of daylight I poked my head over the top for a look. It was a damned silly thing to do, but I couldn't help it. I will never forget what I saw.

The frost made a smoke on the ground. Thick and white, it flowed like a half-frozen river, like slow-moving water. It oozed through the wire, through the craters and pits. Then out of that smoke came the Huns. Such an endless line of men that it didn't seem possible that we could ever stop them. The smoke swirled round their waists, and it turned red in the rising sun. It turned yellow and red like a river of fire. The Huns came marching toward us.

A whistle blew. Up popped the British. The air filled with the crack of rifles. The rattle of machine guns.

The Germans started running. They started running and shouting, all of them together. A terrible moaning and wailing. Their bayonets rose up, sparkling like stars.

I won't say much about the battle. It was fast and brutal, full of screams and flashing silver and redness everywhere. But once it was over, I was sent back to the rear, and I scarcely remember even making the journey. All I recall is the smell of Maconochie's stew warming up on someone's tin-can stove, and the feeling that it had all been only a dream, only a nightmare.

I am a bit weary and rather friendless now. It was a blessing that I could spend the day working on the little man, enclosed, whom I carved from a piece of a shattered gun carriage. He seemed to emerge from the wood just as you see him, as though he'd been buried in there and was waiting for his freedom.

My heart aches to see you again. I fear it might break if I don't get home very soon.

   All my love,
   Dad

The new man was screaming.

His eyes were huge holes, his mouth like a wound. He seemed to be stretching his hands toward the sky, but the way he stood—twisted at the waist—made him even more out of balance than Harry Black had been.

I remembered how the little blacksmith had looked more comfortable when Mr. Tuttle laid him down. So I put the new man on his back, on the tabletop, and I saw it was just the way he was meant to be. He lay in an arch, on his hands and his bottom.

"He's laughing," said Auntie. But she didn't sound as though she believed it. The man was screaming as he writhed on the ground.

"Johnny, he's *laughing,*" she said, more sternly.

I stared at the figure, the most troubling man of them all.

"Do you see what it's like now?" asked Auntie. "Do you see what it's really like?"

"Why are you angry?" I said.

"I'm not," she told me. "Not at you." She reached across the table and patted my wrist. "Johnny, there are men who can go to a war and come home just the same as they were. But not your father. He's a toy maker, Johnny. He spends his life bringing pleasure to people, to children. The war will kill him."

"Don't say that!" I said.

"Oh, on the inside," she cried, and tightened her fingers around my wrist. "Johnny, I just meant on the inside. It will rot him away if it doesn't end soon. He'll be changed; he'll be different. He'll be hollow."

She hadn't met the Highlander, but she might have been talking about him. He'd had no wounds, but something had torn him apart.

Auntie Ivy's thumb rubbed the backs of my fingers.

"Johnny, I'm sorry," she said. "There's nothing wrong with your games if they make you remember your father. When James was a boy he did the same thing when his own father went to the war."

"He played with his little gun," I said, staring at my soldier. "He played Zulus sometimes."

She laughed. "Yes, I was a Zulu once. Who told you about that?"

"The soldier," I said.

"What soldier?"

I shrugged. "He came to the garden. He used to know Dad."

"Everyone did," said Auntie Ivy. "And everyone loved him." She took her hand away. "Now go and play, Johnny."

I didn't feel like fighting my soldiers. But I cleaned up the trenches and put the men in order. Then I made barbed wire from the twine that was left over from my Guy Fawkes guy, laying it out in coils across my no-man's-land. I staked it down with twigs from the beech tree, going back and forth from the trenches to collect them by the wall.

On my third trip there I saw the sergeant watching me. He stood among the trees, in his khaki clothes, and all I saw at first was his face. "Hello," I shouted, but he didn't answer.

I stepped closer, and his arms appeared among the branches. His uniform was tattered now, the collars frayed, the cuffs unraveled. He looked as though he'd walked a hundred miles, through mud and thorns, since I'd seen him last. "Are you all right?" I asked.

He still didn't answer. His mouth opened and closed, and he moved backward, slinking into the forest. Then he turned and started to run, if you could call it that. He went away in a hobbling gait, with one leg stiff, until I couldn't see him anymore.

That night I dreamed about him. I saw him crossing a battlefield in that same hobbling way. I shouted at him, and he turned around. And his face was my father's.

It was snowing when I woke. I lay in my bed watching the flakes spiral past the window. I thought of it snowing in France, all of no-man's-land turning to white. I wanted to see my own battlefield looking like that, but by morning the snow had changed to rain, and there was only a bit of slush on the ground. I went off to school in my Wellingtons, the rubber soles squeaking with every step.

At the post office I met Sarah. She was slogging along, her feet dragging troughs in the slush. When I caught up to her she looked at me, and *her* face was different too. It was like Auntie Ivy's, wrinkled with worry.

"He died," she said.

"Who?"

"My dad." She sniffed, and started sobbing.

"What happened?" I asked.

Her lips quivered. Her breath hissed through her teeth. Every time she tried to speak she started crying instead.

I thought of her father. I remembered how tall he was, how *heroic* he was in his big coat and his polished buttons. I could hear his voice and see his smile, how happy he'd been in the garden. It seemed so real just then that I could remember the smell of the rain on his woolen clothes. It wasn't possible that he was dead, that he was gone—just like that—forever.

"Sarah," I said.

"Yesterday," she said. She sobbed and took a breath. "We got a letter from him yesterday."

She clamped a hand across her face, across her eyes and nose. "He said he was happy. He said he'd been scared but he wasn't anymore. He told us not to worry."

Sarah rubbed her eyes, then took her hand away. She blinked, spilling tears on her cheeks. "He was dead when we got it." Suddenly, she smiled. "Johnny, it was like he wrote it from heaven."

She walked with me for a while, but very slowly. She was like a flower that was wilting; her shoulders slumped, her head drooped down. Then she stopped altogether. "I don't even know how he died," she said. "I don't know what happened to him yet."

Children rushed past us. A ball of slush plopped on the ground at my feet. A boy shouted, laughing, "Johnny's going to get maa-aaried!"

Sarah put her hand on my arm. "You don't think a shell hit him, do you?"

"Maybe." I didn't know what to say. "Do you want to come to Auntie's after school? Do you want to play with my—"

"No," she said. "I won't." She backed away. "I wish I'd never gone there."

"Why?"

She gave me a terrible look. Then she started crying again, harder than before.

"What's wrong?" I said.

She turned and ran. She fled down her trail of ragged footprints, past buildings that were shedding snow from their steep roofs, then round the bend at the edge of the village. I could see the marshes beyond her, white and flat, and imagined her running across them, all the way to the Thames and on to London, on and on for as far as she could go.

I went on to school and sat behind her empty desk. Mr. Tuttle stood at the front of the room in his long black gown. "Children," he said. "We should pray." We bowed our heads and prayed for Sarah's father, for his soul. We prayed for Sarah, for her mother, for all of our fathers who were fighting in France. It was the first time I had done that in school, but it wouldn't be nearly the last.

That same day, in the evening, the lieutenant's name was in the paper. It was listed in the Honor Roll, in the section for the officers, in a little box shaped like a grave. Auntie Ivy pointed it out. "Killed in action," it said beside his name.

"I met him," I said. "I liked him."

"I know you did," said Auntie. There wasn't a bit of news or a single secret in all of Cliffe that Auntie didn't know.

"Then why did he die?"

"Who can say why?" She shook her head. "Not me, not you."

Auntie Ivy made an enormous supper that night, a rabbit stew that she cooked in two pots. I didn't know why until we finished and she put on her coat and her boots.

"I'm taking some food to Mrs. Sims," she said. "Would you like to come?"

"I was going to play with my soldiers," I said.

But Auntie had already made up my mind. "No, I think you'd rather come with me."

It was dark when we got to the farm. In the lane beside the house a lantern was burning, and in its yellowish glow a man was loading wood into a wagon bed. He stood on a pile of split rounds, pitching them up one-handed. His arm seemed to go round and round in circles, catching the wood and hurling it up. The lantern light shone on a hook that he held.

"That's Storey," said Auntie, her voice dropping to a whisper. "He sells firewood around the village." We passed him at a distance as we walked toward the farmhouse. I fancied his hook; it would be a splendid thing for climbing trees or plucking trout from rivers. But Auntie told me: "He lost his hand, you see. It was shot away in the Burma war, and all he's got is a claw."

She walked away and I hurried up behind her. We climbed to the porch, but Auntie didn't knock on the door. She pushed it open and called, "Yoo-hoo!"

Shreds of paper hung above us, tiny scraps of blue and white and red. Warm air, tart with smoke, wafted out through the door, and the bits of paper rustled and coiled. The house felt empty, the air like its breath.

I could hear Mrs. Sims walking across the floor above us. Her voice quavered down: "I'll be right there."

"It's only me," said Auntie.

We walked right in, to a warm and smoky parlor. We stood on the hearth, warming our hands and our fronts at the fire.

"Those are the sons," said Auntie, tipping her head toward a pair of portraits on the mantel. "There's just the two of them, no daughters."

Mrs. Sims was coming down the stairs. Auntie bent

her head and whispered, soft as feathers, "Both the boys went to war. It was Murdoch who was killed."

"Who's the other one?" I asked.

"Hush."

"I know him," I said. But Auntie Ivy had turned away to greet her neighbor.

I took the picture down. I held it out to Mrs. Sims who stopped in midstep. She stared at me from her black veils and her shawls. "Look. He's my friend," I said, smiling. "He comes to the garden. I saw him just the other night."

Mrs. Sims gasped. She touched her forehead, then crumpled to the floor.

"Johnny!" Auntie slapped me on the head. She went running to hold Mrs. Sims. "You wicked boy. That's Murdoch."

Chapter 12

For three days there were no letters from my father. I sat and wrote to him instead, even though it wasn't Friday.

Dear Dad, I wrote. *How are you? I am <u>not</u> fine. Auntie Ivy hit me yesterday just because I said the picture on Mrs. Sims's mantel was a picture of my friend who's a soldier. She hit me so hard that I might have chipped a tooth. The marks of her fingers were still on my cheek when I went to bed and that was a long time later. She called me a monster and*

Auntie Ivy came thumping up behind me. I tried to hide the letter, but she saw it and snatched it away.

"That's mine!" I cried.

She turned aside. It took her only a moment to read the letter, and a moment after that she was stuffing it into the firebox. "You're not going to worry your father with petty things like this," she said. "Chipped a tooth, indeed."

"I might have," I said.

"You got just what you deserved." She put the lid on

the firebox. "You might have stopped her heart; did you think of that? The state she's in, you could have killed her, Johnny."

"But it was true," I said. "That was my soldier in the picture."

"A dead man?" she asked.

"Maybe Murdoch isn't dead."

"Oh, Johnny," she said, heaving a great sigh. "I'll tell you what happened, and then maybe you'll admit you were wrong."

She sat and told me all about Murdoch. It was a cracking good story, but she made it sound as dull as a grammar lesson. "Murdoch's regiment attacked the Germans. They went out and came straggling back. There was no sign of Murdoch for three days, until he was found in a shell crater with a bullet in his leg. He was just four yards from his trench, but he lay there for three days. Then he was carried back to a dressing station, and his parents were sent a telegram saying that he was coming home. They were hanging streamers of bunting in the doorway—to welcome him back—when the postman brought the second telegram, saying that Murdoch had died of his wounds."

"Was he a sergeant?" I asked.

"Yes, he was."

"So was mine," I said. "And I think mine was wounded in the leg, too. He couldn't walk very well."

Auntie Ivy scowled. "Why won't you listen to reason?" she asked. "The next day an officer showed up at Storey's farm, carrying a little package. Murdoch's wallet and identification tag were in it." Auntie Ivy put her fingers round her wrist to show me where Murdoch would have worn his bracelet. "There were a few letters that he had written but had never got around to sending. It was so sad. Such a little parcel, but everything the poor boy owned."

"Everything?"

"Yes." Auntie leaned forward, and a look of kindness came to her face for the first time since she had slapped me. "Now don't you see that you have to be wrong? There's no way on God's earth that Murdoch could have come to the garden, is there?"

"No, Auntie," I said.

"Are you sorry?"

"Yes."

"Well, it's a little late for sorries." She stood up, her chair squeaking. "You've put it into poor old Storey's head that his son is still alive. You should be ashamed of yourself."

She didn't speak to me for the rest of that day. She ate supper in silence, then sent me to bed by pointing her finger.

The night was crisp and clear. By morning, I thought, there might be frost on the ground. I lay in bed and watched the moon come up through the branches of the beech tree. I heard the guns in France.

They were faint but furious, a steady drumming of low-pitched pops and puffs. It was strange to think that such a harmless sound meant that the ground was shaking where my father was, that all the earth around him would be churning like a stormy sea, and the air would be full of razors. I didn't know if the guns were German or British. For all I knew they might have been both, firing together, hurling shells back and forth in the darkness, like giants playing at pitch-and-toss.

The moon was bright enough to cast shadows on my wall. The branches of the beech tree made patterns there, of loops and crosses, like the writing on my father's letters. I saw them, and thought again how long it had been since he had sent anything to me. I wondered if it was true what Auntie had said, if he was already rotting away on the inside, if he had already forgotten about me.

I got up and stood at the window. I looked toward France, or where I thought France was. The guns popped and puffed, but I couldn't see any flashes of light, or any sign that they were really there.

Below me were my wooden soldiers. The nutcracker men were hidden in the dark shadows of the tree and the wall, but the moonlight gleamed on my Frenchmen and my Tommies, as ghastly as the star shells my father had written about. I could see him in the garden, his model. It was tipped back in the trench, staring up at the sky, paler than ever in the white of the moon. The guns in France pounded away with their faint little thunder, and I thought that my real dad would be just like my model, wide awake, watching the sky.

I went down to the garden in my grandfather's robe. The mud had a thin, cold crust that shattered as I walked across it. My boots echoed the sounds of the guns.

All that night I shelled the German trenches. I bombarded the nutcracker men with pebbles and dirt and mud until my hands were black and stiff. The moon went down and I kept at it. The nutcracker men became real in my mind. They became the Hun, and I blasted away with my shells, angry at all the things they had caused. They had driven me from London; they had taken my dad away and were rotting him inside; they had killed Sarah's dad and Murdoch Sims. And I punished them for all of that.

The eastern sky turned a dismal gray. Dawn was coming, and I launched my attack.

I whistled my Tommies over the top. I whistled again for my Frenchmen. My father and the dog-faced man, the sergeant and my messman, all my Pierres and all my Tommies rose from the mud two at a time. They gathered on the edge of no-man's-land, then marched forward in little bunches as I pushed them along.

It was hard in the darkness, all by myself. The battles had been fast and furious when Sarah had helped me. My army had stormed along then, but now it just plodded.

When the men reached the wire I stepped across them to the German line. Fatty Dienst peered over the parapet. *"Mein Gott!"* he said. "The Tommies are coming!"

The nutcracker men stood up to their guns. I hurled some dirt across them, moved the British forward, and let the machine guns open fire.

"Ratta-tatta-tat!" I swiveled the little Germans in my fingers, spraying the British with bullets. I knocked down the dog-faced soldier.

General Cedric stood on a bump of mud that covered a stone. "I can't see what's happening," he said. "Are we winning?"

The British moved forward. My father slid down to a crater and up the other side. "Follow me!" he shouted.

The mud was frozen in clusters, in little honeycombs

of white and gray. It crackled under my boots as I moved back and forth from the Germans to the British.

"Whizz. Bang!" A bit of German trench collapsed. "Ratta-tatta-tatta!" The messman with his silly pots spun around and fell.

My father reached the wire. He hopped over it, then reeled in my fingers. "Come on, lads!"

The others stumbled up behind him, and past him, tangling in my bits of string. A few shells came down, shattering among the men. I whistled again, and the Tommies carried on, the sergeant at the front. They straggled across all of no-man's-land.

"Fall back!" shouted Fatty Dienst.

But the Germans held the line, because Auntie Ivy came and saved them. She rushed from the house in her nightgown, with a broom in her hand. "Who's there?" she cried. "Who's out there?"

It wasn't light enough that she could see me in the shadows near the wall. She shouted again—"Who's there?"—then came down the steps with her broom held up like a lance, ready to chase off whatever person or thing that she found.

I stood up. I felt like a soldier surrendering. "It's me," I said.

"Johnny?" She didn't stop until she stood right in front of me. "Are you out of your mind? Have you lost your senses?"

"I was only playing," I said.

"In the dead of night? In your pajamas no less?" She was even angrier than she'd been at Storey's farm. She swatted at me with her broom. "Shoo!"

I stood away, staggering over the battlefield. The broom swished past behind me, swished again, and mowed down a dozen soldiers. Auntie swept them away like bits of dirt, like rubbish. She sent them scattering left and right, then chased me back to the house.

I was shivering from the cold. Auntie Ivy stoked the fire until the stovepipe hummed. She heated a kettle and washed the mud from my shaking hands, from my face and my arms. She pulled off my boots and plunged my feet into a basin of steaming hot water. Then she wrapped me up in a tent of blankets, muttering all the time about the stupidity of boys.

"Thank goodness your mother can't see you now," she said.

The steam and the blasting heat of the stove made me tired. I could have slept the day away, but it seemed that I had barely closed my eyes when Auntie shook me awake again. She pulled the blankets away, and sunlight hurt my eyes.

"You'd better get dressed, Johnny," she said. "You'll be late for school if you don't get a move on."

Her anger had left her. She hummed as she worked, bending over the stove. The oven door clanked open, and I saw a sheet of browned scones that might have appeared there by magic. She plucked one out, split it and smeared it with butter, then thrust it into my hands. I had to juggle it from one to another, and nearly burnt my tongue when I took the first bite.

I walked to school through a land that was white with frost. Everything sparkled and glittered, and the air was as crisply cool as peppermints. It was the first wintery day, and the thought of that gave me a little thrill of pleasure. In a few weeks Christmas would come, the war would end and my dad would be home.

For the first time in days I saw Sarah at school. I came into class a few minutes late to see her sitting at her desk. I sat down, reached forward, and tapped her on the shoulder.

"Hello," I said when she turned around.

That look came back to her eyes, that same dark and terrible stare that she'd given me the last time I'd seen her. "Don't touch me," she said, too loudly. Everyone looked at us; even Mr. Tuttle stopped pacing and stared toward us.

Sarah glared at me. "It was that game," she said. "That stupid game."

I didn't understand her then. But I knew exactly what she meant as soon as I went home in the afternoon.

Auntie Ivy was knitting her socks. "You look miserable," she said.

I sat down and watched the wool twisting through her needles, knotting itself into rows of stitches.

"Was Sarah at school?" asked Auntie.

"Yes," I said.

"The poor thing." Auntie shook her head, but didn't stop knitting. "If it's any consolation, Johnny, her father wouldn't have felt a thing. It was sudden." She glanced up as she tugged at her wool. "He was hit by a shell."

Into my mind flew a picture of my wooden lieutenant, the mud from Sarah's boots spraying against him, flinging him sideways. *It was that game. That stupid game.*

Goose bumps came up on my arm. I rubbed them, but couldn't take the coldness away. "Auntie," I said. "Do you think my soldiers might have killed him?"

She put her knitting down. "Your *wooden* soldiers?"

"Yes," I said. "If we pretended one was him? If it fell and—"

"No!" she said. "Oh, Johnny, that's silly; that's non-sense."

"Even if it looked like him?"

"Oh, goodness, no." She sounded sad. "You can't take the world on your shoulders. Dear Johnny. You're so sweet, and so stupid as well."

She dropped her wool on the floor and made me stand beside her. She touched my back with a cold, hard hand. "If you could wish someone dead, if you could really do that, I would have gone to my grave the first day you saw me."

"But I didn't *wish* him dead," I told her.

"Did you kill all those soldiers in the Honor Roll? Did you kill all the ones from yesterday, and the ones from the day before?"

"No, Auntie," I said.

"Did you kill Murdoch Sims?"

"I don't even know him," I said.

"You see?" Her eyes were nearly level with mine. They looked like old glass, all cloudy inside. "It had nothing to do with you."

I went outside and sat under the beech tree. I looked at my soldiers strewn about, the wounded from my battle, the ones that Auntie's broom had scattered far and wide. Only the nutcracker men, deep in their trenches, were still where I'd left them. They had their backs toward me, their bayonets raised. *Those are very special soldiers, those*, my father had said. Mr. Tuttle had told me that they were almost alive. And who had said they had souls?

I found an old beechnut, softened by rain, and threw it at the little Germans. They were only wood, I told myself. That was all they were, just wood.

I threw another nut. It bounced over no-man's-land. I thought of the broken Pierre, shattered by a shell. I could see the pebble that marked his grave, and beyond it the ambulance that had come in the post as though to fetch him from the battlefield. I remembered my sleeping man, and the terrible shelter that my real dad had found during a trench raid that was so much like mine. A prickly feeling shot through me.

Suddenly the garden seemed haunted by all the things that I'd done, by the battles that I'd fought. I heard the patter of machine guns and the boom of muddy shells, the clear call of my little brass whistle. I heard Sarah shouting, her father laughing. Then I saw him in France. I saw him raising his hands as he heard the shell coming down. He must have known, for an instant, that it would land right beside him. He must have known that it would *splatter* him into pieces.

The prickly feeling got worse. I closed my eyes, but I couldn't shut out that picture of Sarah's dad as the shell came screaming down.

"They're only wood!" I shouted.

I crawled across the battlefield, searching for the little man with his tiny rifle. I picked up the soldiers one by one, pulling them from craters, from the roots of the tree. One was half buried, another head down in a puddle. My dad was wrapped up in the wire, a big coil of the string twisted around him, like a thing that a spider had caught.

Nearly all his paint was gone, and the little knothole in his chest looked bigger and darker. The split was a tiny bit wider, a tiny bit longer. The dugout I'd made him was ruined, destroyed by the shelling or by Auntie's broom. So I put him into the trench with the others.

"He's all right," said the bellowing sergeant.

But deep in my heart I was afraid for my dad.

CHAPTER 13

December 13, 1914

Dearest Johnny,

Just a very quick note to let you know that I'm thinking about you always. If anything should happen to me, and for some reason I don't get back to see you for a long, long time, then I want you to remember that I think the whole world of you, son.

Of course you don't know this, but many nights when you were young I stood in your doorway and watched you sleep. I tried to imagine what you would be like as a man. I tried to think what you would look like and where you would live and what sort of fellow you would be. But try as I might, I could never see you as anything more than a boy.

Well, last night I dreamed of you as a man. You were standing above me, looking down at the spot where I was lying. I had been lying there for a long time, and I understood that you had come to visit several times. I knew that you were successful and happy, that you had a wife and children of your own. I ached to reach up and touch your hand, to tell you not to cry at the thought of me lying there under the ground.

Oh, Johnny, I just want to tell you how terribly proud I am to be your father. I love you more than words can say.

Enclosed is a soldier with a shovel. It's his job to see that we're comfortable in the end.

Bless you, Johnny. Don't ever forget how much I love you.
Dad

The letter came in a special green envelope covered with postage marks. There was a note on the front that Dad had signed, saying it contained nothing but private matters.

Auntie tore it open. Right away the soldier tumbled out, the shovel in his hands. We thought he was digging trenches. We thought it was maybe my father, working through his period of rest. Then Auntie read the letter, and her voice grew fainter and fainter, until I barely heard the ending.

I stared at the soldier, at the shovel in his hands. He wasn't digging, but the blade was in the ground, and he was leaning on the handle. His head was bent down, and he looked terribly sad, all hunched at the shoulders.

Auntie Ivy looked at him, then burst into tears.

I went out to a garden that was still covered with soldiers. They lay on their sides and their backs and their bellies, a scene of slaughter that I would have loved at one time, but that now only shocked me.

I tried to pretend that my new man was just digging out trenches. He went to work with my other shoveling man, clearing the rubble from my battle. "Give us room," he shouted. "Fritz has made a proper mess of everything here."

But he leaned on his shovel, and I couldn't forget that he was really a grave digger. I moved him to the rear trenches, then farther back again. I moved him so far from the battle that he might have been in England.

Then I brought up the ambulance. It drove through the scattered men, stopping here and there as I piled the soldiers on top. I drove by mistake right over the messman, who tipped on his side, his arm reaching up. Again the ambulance stopped, but there was no more room on the roof.

"Never mind him," said the driver. "That one's a goner."

He started off; the motor puttered. He was nearly at Charing Cross when I heard the ring of a bicycle bell. It brought my head up with a start, that sound like the telegraph machine. My ambulance tipped over, spilling my soldiers.

The bell rang again, a little louder and closer. I thought of the postman pedaling along, carrying his message from cold Mr. Death.

I stood up. No one lived farther from Cliffe than Auntie Ivy. There was only empty road to the south, all the way to the railway station.

The bell jangled.

"Go past," I said to myself. "Oh, please, make him go past. Don't let him stop here."

But he did. The postman shouted out, "Hello!" and the bell jangled again. "Ivy! Hello."

I got up from the mud, staggered and fell. My barbed wire snagged on my boot, and I kicked it off. I stomped over the battlefield, over the trenches; I ran from the garden, around to the front as Auntie Ivy came thumping down the steps.

In the middle of the road stood the old postman, holding his bicycle at a slant. In his hand was a sheet of paper the color of biscuits.

"Go away!" shrieked Auntie Ivy. She raced through the gate and battered against the postman. His bicycle crashed to the ground. "Keep going," she screamed. "Go on!"

He caught her in his arms, the paper crumpling. "It's news," he said. "It's great news."

Auntie Ivy held on to his shoulder. She was crying.

"I'm telling everyone," said the postman. "I'm making the rounds, and now I'm going to have the church bells rung."

"For mercy's sake, why?" asked Auntie Ivy.

"A victory!" The old postman danced her in a jig. "There's been a great victory in France."

I felt almost a shock. "Is it over?" I asked.

"No. Lord, no," said the postman. "But we pushed the Germans back. All along the line." He picked up his bicycle and rang the bell. Then he leaned across it and kissed my auntie on the cheek.

"Gracious," she said.

"Must be off." He swung his leg over the bar and went weaving down the road, giving his bell one last jingle.

Auntie Ivy looked at me. "You're white as a sheet," she said. "It's all right, Johnny. It was only news."

My knees were trembling. "Auntie," I said. "I think I might have done it."

"Done what?" she asked.

"The victory," I told her. "I had a battle with my soldiers. I pushed the Germans back, and now it's really happened. I think it's—"

"What rubbish!" she said.

"But, Auntie," I said. "It happened before. When Dad went over the top my soldier did too."

"This is nonsense," she said. "This is utter nonsense."

She started off toward the house, and I grabbed her purple dress. "Just listen," I said.

"I don't listen to rubbish." She knocked my hand away and kept on going.

"Auntie!" I cried.

"Those are wooden soldiers you've got in the garden," she said. "Just little wooden soldiers."

I ran in front of her, but she swept on by. Her shoes went thunk and thunk beside me. Again I grabbed her dress, and dragged her to a stop.

"Let me go," she said.

"What if it's true?" I asked.

"Johnny Briggs, I thought you had some sense," she said. "I thought you were smarter than that." She wrenched her dress from my hands and thumped up the steps to the house.

I went back to the garden. My barbed wire was pulled away, a bit of trench ruined where I'd fallen. And there, smashed into the ground, was the little model of my father. As gray as the frost, his face stared up from the dirt.

"Oh, no," I said. "No!" He looked like a corpse.

Far away, the church bell tolled. It was a single deep "bong" of a sound, softened by the distance. It tolled again, and then a third time, and I pictured that enormous bell swinging faster in its great stone steeple. I saw, in my mind, the postman clinging to the rope, using all his weight to drag it down, letting it lift him up, clear from the floor. The bell tolled and tolled.

I dropped to my knees. I plucked the wooden man from the ground, but only half his body came away. The crack that had opened down his middle now split him into two.

I felt such a rush of dread that it made me almost dizzy. I snatched up the pieces and rushed to the house, shouting for my auntie. She came lumbering into the kitchen, and found me weeping at the door.

She stared at my hands and scowled. "Here I thought you'd gone and broken your arm," she said. "And it's only a toy. What a fuss to make over a wooden toy."

I held it out in my cupped hands. They were shaking, and the halves of the figure knocked together. "It's my dad," I sobbed. "He's broken in two and I'm afraid he's dead."

"Oh, Johnny," she said. She put her hands around mine, her fingers like icicles. She squeezed very gently. "It doesn't mean anything. Really it doesn't."

I sniffed and cried. "What if he's dead?" I asked. "What if I killed him?"

"You haven't." She stooped down until our eyes were level. "Do you hear me? It's just a piece of wood. Nothing more than that."

"I have to fix him," I said. "Auntie, I've got to."

"Then I'll get the glue pot."

"Hurry!" I shouted.

It might have been the first time in her life that my Auntie Ivy sat down on the floor. With her dress all puddled around her, her legs tucked underneath, she looked as though she *had* no legs, or as though she'd sunken through the floor. She put on her tiny spectacles and took the soldier from me.

"We'll fix him up," she said. "Then we'll put a bandage on him so the glue will set."

Her hands trembled. Her eyes squinted behind her tiny specs, and her mouth squashed in until I saw her teeth and gums.

I leaned forward, watching Auntie smear the wood with glue. She pressed the pieces together.

"They're crooked!" I cried.

She straightened them out. Beads of glue squirted from the wood, bubbling along the crack like pus from a wound. In the distance, a second bell joined in with the first, and then a third as the ringers arrived at the church. The halves of my wooden man came together perfectly, just as the bells rang a wonderful chime, a beautiful chorus.

Auntie Ivy wrapped the man in gauze, slipped a pin through the bandage, then passed him to me. He felt fragile and light, as though weak from the wounds.

"Thank you," I said. The bells went on and on, their sounds flowing on top of each other, cascading down like musical rivers.

"We should have a celebration." Auntie stood up, all her bones popping. "In honor of the victory. I'll make a cake and we'll have a splendid supper."

"But I have to go to Mr. Tuttle's house," I told her. "You know it's Saturday."

"Invite him!" She fiddled with the glue pot, pressing the lid into place. "We'll have chicken, I think."

"Really? A chicken?" My mouth watered at the thought of that rare treat. "It's not even Christmas yet."

"But we have to celebrate," said Auntie Ivy. "And poor Mr. Tuttle will have to fend for himself if you don't want him to come."

"I suppose I can ask him," I said.

She smiled. "All right. If that's what you want."

I took the wooden man back to the garden. As the bells chimed, I stood him in the trench. The other soldiers cheered to see him back, and Dad laughed and said, "No fear, lads. I'm right as rain. I wasn't hurt at all."

But I worried about him—about my real father. I could see the spot in the old German line where his wooden figure had raided the trenches. *I went over the top last night, and I'm quivering in my boots this morning to think what a narrow escape I had.* Farther down the garden was the place where Pierre had been smashed by a stone, the spot where his body had appeared in the mud. *The most astonishing things sometimes turn up when the parapet collapses.*

The bells stopped, their last chime a tingling echo. It seemed that the whole war had gone like that. I remembered marching my nutcracker soldiers across the floor when they had no army to fight. Then Dad had given me a Tommy, and Britain had joined the war. He'd given me more Tommies, and Frenchmen, and soon the real Germans had fallen back at the Marne.

That feeling of goose bumps came back to me. It seemed that whatever I did with my nutcracker men would happen soon after in France. And I looked at my father, split down the middle, and felt sick all over again.

But I had *meant* to raid the trenches. I had *meant* to push the Germans back. And breaking the figure was only an accident. Maybe accidents didn't count.

I wondered if I should take the little soldier to Mr. Tuttle's house. It might keep my real dad safe if I took the model from the trenches. It might even bring him home, I thought, if I took that wooden soldier far enough away. The distance to Mr. Tuttle's house would be a hundred miles or more to him. Then I smiled and picked up the wooden man. And I stopped again.

What if I took the toy away and my father disappeared? What if he went "missing in action" like all the others in the paper? So I put him back in the trenches, and went off to see Mr. Tuttle.

I found him behind his house, staring at the roses. He heard me coming and turned around. "Oh, Johnny," he said. He sounded disappointed.

"Are you waiting for someone?" I asked.

"Always," he said. "Every day I think a boy will surely come and make his confession. But I'm afraid my die is cast." He stepped up to his roses, and his hand went out and took the tips of their branches. "In just a few weeks I'll be done with the classroom, and perhaps with Cliffe as well."

"Why?"

"They're not pulling through." He squeezed the branches, then his hand fell away. "But enough of that. You've come for your lesson, of course."

"And something else," I said. "Auntie's cooking chicken. To celebrate the victory. She'd like you to come."

"She would?"

"Yes, sir. You could see my soldiers, too."

"The crowning glory. Well, thank you, Johnny." He bowed like a lord. "I accept your invitation."

He was happier than I'd ever seen him, so happy that

he canceled our lesson. He was still smiling that evening, when he came to the door in his overcoat and old gray suit.

Our supper was cooking, and Auntie Ivy was setting the table with her best china. Mr. Tuttle sniffed at the wonderful odors that came from the kitchen. "It smells like ambrosia," he said.

"Oh, mercy no," said Auntie Ivy, blushing. "It's only chicken."

Mr. Tuttle was nearly half again her height. Beside her, he looked tall and nearly handsome.

"It will be another half hour," she told me. "You'll have to entertain your visitor."

I took him outside, and he gazed down—grinning— at the little soldiers. "What an army," he said. "It makes me feel like Zeus to stand above them like this."

"They had a fierce battle," I said. "The Germans were pushed back all along the front."

I was hoping he would say, "That's just what happened in France." But he only peered at the men. "Why is that fellow bandaged?" he asked. "Are you pretending that there's something wrong with him?"

He made me feel small. To him, I was only playing with toy soldiers. He didn't know there was so much more than that.

"Is your little man wounded?" he asked.

"No," I said.

"Is he sick?"

"There's nothing wrong with him."

Mr. Tuttle looked puzzled, and I knew he could never understand. Sarah had already guessed what my wooden men could do, but Mr. Tuttle never would. It was the sort of thing that adults wouldn't believe.

An hour later, we were sitting down to a supper that was the nicest I'd had in Cliffe.

Mr. Tuttle and Auntie Ivy talked about the school and the church and the minister. They made me think of my parents, and our suppers before the war. Auntie Ivy kept looking at Mr. Tuttle in the same way that my mother would look at my father. She passed him potatoes and peas and more and more chicken. And we never once talked about the victory in France. It was as though there wasn't a war at all.

Chapter 14

December 15, 1914

Dearest Johnny,

You may have heard by now that we launched a huge attack against the Huns. Well, the funniest thing happened to me.

It started with the usual barrage, that whine and thump of shells that sets my nerves tingling. I was in the rear when the first round went off, and the air seemed torn in two. All that day I listened to it, and watched the earth heave and churn. At night I moved up to the front, into a trench that was so packed with men that we stood shoulder to shoulder, with nothing to do but wait for the appointed hour to arrive. The bit of sky that we could see pulsed with dim flashes of light.

As dawn approached, the sky grew lighter. I saw the faces of the men beside me, and then of those beside them, and then of more and more and more. Each man seemed utterly alone, looking up at the sky or down at the ground. Some of them prayed. Some exchanged letters and little packets of pictures. And the time for our attack, that appointed hour, crept closer and closer.

We got our tot of rum. We knocked it back. The lieutenants stood up on the raised platform. In their neat brown uniforms, their darker hats, they looked like sparrows hopping there. Each wore a silver whistle at his neck, a pistol at his belt. And the time came closer, just moments away.

The guns stopped, and the silence was dreadful. We fixed our bayonets with a clack of metal, a sound that rippled through a mile of trenches, from thousands and thousands of rifles. Just seconds to wait.

Wooden ladders lifted up and fell in place. The lieutenants hopped up on the rungs. Their whistles blew like shrill, clear chirps. And up we went in a horde of men, in a roar of cheers and shouts.

I was one of the first. I clambered from the trench, slipped, and rose again. Then I found my feet, and for as far as I could see on either side there were others rising from the trench, surging forward. It seemed that they came from the earth, that the mud was shaping itself into men. And we went forward, shoulder to shoulder across the no-man's-land.

The rising sun glittered on our bayonets. It shone along the coils of wire. And it was a glorious thing to be there, to be marching against the Hun with twenty thousand comrades. I plodded along, full of this sense of power, of being part of a huge and glorious thing. We'd been told not to run, but it was all I could do to keep my step with the others, to hold myself back. I cheered and shouted.

And then the shelling started. The shelling and machine guns. Great holes opened in the air, to be filled with whumps and shrieks and howls of the most unearthly sort. Our line wavered and carried on, like a row of grass that the wind had torn across. Gaps appeared and closed again. The men that had come from the earth settled back to the earth. They just laid themselves down and didn't get up.

I reached the wire. It was meant to be shattered by the barrage, but there it stood, in coils and thickets as strong as ever. It grabbed my ankles and pulled me down. It grabbed my hands as I struggled to free myself.

Men went stepping past me. Bullets whistled all around. There were smoke and thumps and mud splashed up across me. And I rolled and twisted in the wire. Then someone pulled me free, and someone took my other arm, and they swept me up. It seemed they pulled me through the wire, that they shredded me in two and joined me on the other side.

No one was marching anymore. Everyone was running, some without rifles, some without boots. We raced along, through craters, over mud. I saw the lip of the trench ahead, fire bursting from machine gun mouths. We stepped up to the parapet and hurled ourselves over the edge, tumbling down to the platform, down to the ooze of mud and water. I looked up and saw soldiers all around me, men in British khaki.

I marveled that we'd taken the trench and driven the Germans off. I cheered for the great victory. I was amazed at first how much old Fritz's trench looked just like ours. And then I realized that it was ours. I'd only been turned around in the smoke and the madness, and I was back where I'd started, in the same old ditch I'd left.

It's rather a grand joke, don't you think?

A few men crossed the wire. Even fewer reached the German line. But I got farther than most, and the whole thing was a miserable failure, a lash-up of the worst sort.

Oh, Johnny. My dear Johnny. It's plain to me now that I won't be home for Christmas this year. Perhaps not for the

*next, but we shan't worry about that right now. I'm sorry
to let you down, but I hope you'll understand.*

*Enclosed is a small figure. If he looks a bit odd, it's
because my hands were shaking rather badly.*

All my love, forever and ever,
Dad

Auntie Ivy put the letter down. She didn't move for a
long time; then she trembled once, and wiped her eyes.
"You see?" she said, and tried to smile. "Your father's
fine, Johnny. You worried over nothing."

"But is he still all right?" I asked.

She frowned.

"Is he?" I pulled at the paper that was wrapped round
and round the newest soldier. "He didn't write that letter
this morning. Yesterday they had the victory. Maybe yesterday he was—"

"Don't say it," she said. "Don't even think it, Johnny."

"But, Auntie. This wasn't a victory. It was just a big
mess." I tore off a layer of wrapping. "And the newspaper
said it was a great victory."

"Maybe the newspapers got it wrong," said Auntie.
"It wouldn't be the first time, would it?"

"I think the letters haven't caughten up," I said.

"Caughten up," she scoffed. "Don't let Mr. Tuttle hear
you say that."

"But how can I know?" I said. "How can I know he's
all right?"

"Because he is," she said. "Because he always is and
always will be. I just won't stand for you thinking anything else."

"But—"

I shredded the paper, and the man tumbled out.

"Auntie!" I cried.

It was horrid and twisted, a tortured little man. Auntie Ivy gasped as it rolled across the table.

"Dear mercy," she breathed.

It seemed to twitch on the table, its arms groping out, its legs all disarrayed. It looked awful, barely human, like something from a nightmare.

"Give me that," said Auntie Ivy. She stood up and snatched it away. "That's not fit for a boy to play with."

"Do you think he really saw a man like that?" I asked.

"There's no one like that," she said. "It's not natural." Then she swished across the kitchen, and pried the lid from the firebox.

"You're going to burn it?" I said.

"I certainly am."

I didn't argue. The thing was more horrid than maggots, more horrid than leeches or great, hairy spiders. I felt a huge relief when Auntie Ivy flung it in among the coals.

She took up the poker and stirred the fire into shimmering flames that cast a red pall across her face. She thrust and hammered with it, now at the center, now at the corners, and I imagined that thing crawling inside, squirming away from the poker. Then she slammed the lid down, and the fire crackled and spat.

"I *hate* this war," she said. "Oh, Johnny, I wish it would end."

She started crying, and I had never seen her cry before. It wasn't like the proud, silent tears my mother had shed at the sight of my father in his uniform. It was ghastly and frightening, for she shook all over, as though she'd knock herself to pieces. She covered her face with her hands, but still she kept shaking. And then she shrieked like a bird that had been caught by a cat.

I ran to her. I buried my face in the warm thickness of her purple dress, with the bones of her hip like axe blades chopping at my fingers. She thought I was soothing her, but I was soothing myself. It scared me to see a grown lady cry.

Slowly, she collected herself. She touched me with her cold, thin fingers: on my shoulder; on my neck. "I'm glad you're here, Johnny," she said.

"Why?" I asked.

"I'd feel so alone without you."

"But you're always alone," I said.

"Then lonely, I mean." She pushed her fingers into my hand. "I get so lonely sometimes. So scared of the war. It's nice to have someone with me when everything becomes too much."

I nodded against her; I knew what she meant.

"It's such a terrible war. Men dying in ditches; men falling in rows to machine guns. I'll go mad if it lasts very long, Johnny. I'll go stark staring mad if it does."

She started sobbing again, and I held her. "Don't worry," I said. "The war won't last very long. Not anymore."

Slowly, she stopped crying. "You're a fine boy," she said. "Thank you for everything, Johnny." She patted my back. "Now go off and play; I'll be all right."

I went out to the garden, to my armies in the mud. The sun shone across the ground, but didn't touch my nutcracker men deep in their trenches. They stood in puddles of water, in dark slits of shadows. It made me think of my father and what he had written, not in his last letter but one before, that all he would see from dawn to dusk was the bit of sky above him.

I bent back my head and looked straight up, through the branches of the beech tree. The clouds were gray blotches tumbling past to the east, as scattered as cows in a field. They dotted the sky with shifting shapes, with slowly passing fancies.

I put my hands against my eyes. I made a narrow slit from my fingers and my palms. And the huge field of clouds narrowed to a single furrow, to one lone cloud that bubbled against the blue like paint being swirled in a can. It became a dragon, breathing smoke. Then it passed and another came, a palace with feathery turrets. And I wondered what I would see if I watched long enough. Would I ever see God? His bearded face torn by the wind? His hand reaching down, stretching far to the south, to stir His nest of fighting men?

The thought seemed huge and scary. And suddenly I was frightened that I *would* see God, or that He'd see me, so tiny, staring up. Would it anger Him, I wondered, to find me watching, like a face at a window?

I took my hands down. The passing clouds had made me dizzy, and the trenches of soldiers seemed to turn round the garden. In the middle was the little model of my father, tipped back in the mud, gazing not at the clouds but at me. In his wooden eyes, if he could see, I would be as large as God, filling the sky.

I had never thought of that before, that I was a sort of god to my little soldiers, the savior of the metal Tommies,

the lord of the nutcracker men. I could stir them up how-
ever I wanted, and kill them all if I cared. And maybe it
was true that whatever happened in the garden happened
in faraway France. "Those are very special soldiers,
those," I said.

I looked down at my armies, at the Tommies and the
Frenchmen; I glared at the long row of nutcracker men.
They were more like toys than any of the others, but their
silver helmets, their gnashing teeth, made them furious
and wicked. I found a stone and threw it at them.

I threw another, and another, and when I'd run out of
stones I threw handfuls of mud. I nearly buried the
trench, then dug it out and started again. The nutcracker
men fell on their backs, on their sides; they were blasted
right out of the trench.

I pressed the mud into balls, into nine-pounder shells.
And they burst when I threw them, into tiny bits of
shrapnel that skittered across the mud. And the sun went
down as I hurled my shells, as I grunted with the effort.

It was cold enough that the mud felt like ice on my
fingers, and froze my hands into claws. It was quiet
enough that I heard a flock of rooks cackling in the
woods. The sun blazed crimson across the fields of Kent.

In France, my father would be standing to his gun.
Right then, he'd be stepping up to the platform, laying his
rifle on the sandbags of his parapet, and that same crimson fire would be burning behind him.

I didn't shout or make the sounds of the shells. I just
kept on going, stooping to scrape up the mud, standing to
throw it. The sun-fire dwindled away, and the moon
came up, bright as a lantern, and I hurled my shells in a

silvery darkness where the only sound was the little thump of them hitting.

I had scraped a huge crater all around me when the sergeant appeared, leaning on the wall. He looked older by years, by centuries. His uniform was torn to shreds in places, and he seemed to have shrunk inside it. His cap was crushed, his face a shadow that I couldn't see. He shivered behind the wall, then groaned—a long, sad moan.

My little wooden dad, split in two and joined again, stood not far from him, in a crease in the trench that kept him safe from my bursting shells. He was still bandaged round the waist, and he looked as gray and battered as the soldier at the wall.

"Is that James there?" the sergeant asked. I nodded. "You're keeping him safe," said the sergeant. "Is that what you're doing?"

"Yes," I said.

"You're like the angel standing there. Silvered by the moon."

"What angel?" I asked.

"The Angel of Mons."

I had heard of that, early in the war. Hundreds of soldiers had seen that vision.

"He was huge, Johnny." The sergeant talked in a voice that was like the whisper of wind in winter's trees. "A fiery angel tall as a church; taller, even. He formed from the clouds with the sunbeams shining through him."

The sergeant turned his head up to the moon. It was a white blotch cracked by the shadows of the beech-tree branches. "I was lying on the ground, in a field of grass.

The Huns were only yards away. And I saw him there."
His arm reached up. "A flaming sword in his fist, his
wings all wreathed with fire. He turned the Germans
back; he stopped them in their rush for Mons."

"Did he save you?" I asked.

"He saved us all. He saved the war."

The sergeant was more like a spirit than a person.
The moonlight made him seem unreal and pale as water.
He lowered his arm, and it shook against the stones.

"I didn't want to die," he said, and groaned. "What
have I done that I should suffer like this?"

He terrified me. The mud shells dropped from my
hands. I glanced at the house and took a step backward,
too frightened to turn my back.

"No!" said the sergeant. "Don't leave me." He groped
through his pockets, through his tunic and trousers,
spilling the things that he found in a row on the stones.
As his head tilted down, the moonlight shone past the
peak of his cap, onto his cheeks and their thin, pale
whiskers. His face was gaunt and bony, and I was sure it
was Murdoch; I *knew* it was Murdoch.

He waved me toward him, but I didn't move.

"Johnny, please." He winced and lurched sideways.
His hands grabbed at his leg. Then he closed his eyes for
a moment, and when he opened them again there were
tears dribbling down to his whiskers.

"Look, Johnny. Take what you want." He swept his
hands across the things on the wall. "Take it all if you
want."

I could see a penknife, his pipe, a handkerchief
wadded and dark. His hands went back to his pockets,
back to the wall. Something glittered as he set it down,

and I took a step closer. His identification tag lay on the stones, its chain broken open.

"Take it," he told me.

I went to the wall and reached out for that tag. It had polished itself in his pocket until the metal glistened and shone. I touched it, and his hand clamped onto mine. He held me there, and I was too scared to shout.

"If you take that, you can't tell how you got it. You can't tell anyone."

His hand was colder than the mud. It was bruised and scarred.

He pressed on my hand. "You never saw me. I was never here." Then he snatched up his pipe and his handkerchief, and he stuffed them back in his pockets as he stepped away, turning. He went off in his shuffling limp, off among the dark trees of the forest; in moments he had vanished.

I ran the other way, across the garden and into the house. "He was here," I shouted.

Auntie Ivy came out from the parlor. "Who was here?" she asked. "Not Mr. Tuttle?"

"Murdoch," I told her.

"Gracious!" Her black shoes banged on the floor as she ran to the window, faster than I would have thought possible. "Where?" she said.

"He's gone now," I said. "But he stood right there." I pointed through the window, into the garden. "He told me about the angel, how the angel saved him."

"There's nobody there," she said, her temper rising.

"And he gave me this!" I cried, holding out the silver tag.

It dangled on my fingers, swinging from its chain. I let it slow as Auntie stared at it, her eyes agog.

She took it from me, got her specs and put them on. The metal twinkled as she held it near the light. "Well," she said. "Johnny, you're a simpleton."

The name on the tag was Thomas Cade.

CHAPTER 15

December 17, 1914

Dearest Johnny,

I am sorry that I have been writing such miserable letters lately. I would do anything at all to turn back the clock and take back that carving I sent, that dreadful crawling creature. I must have been off my head to do that, and I have been kicking myself ever since to think of the distress I must have caused you. It was one thing to set out to tell you the truth about the war, but another thing altogether to weigh you down with all my fears and worries.

I'm sure your auntie has already taken away my horrid man, so I won't ask her to do it. One day I'll tell you what inspired me to make that figure, but I think that day can wait until I'm home again, and for a long time afterward too.

You can rest assured that I am no longer in any danger. The war seems to have settled into a bit of a lull, so I'm back to watching the sky. I spend hours at it, I'm afraid. It sounds rather like an utter waste of time, but all of us find endless interest in the clouds. The little wispy ones make us think of bedsheets and flannel. The puffy ones of rabbits. And the big bubbling ones, the thunderheads, take on all manner of shapes. It's like having a lantern show up in the sky, but a magical one where you'll see whatever slides you care to see. Just now there's one of you.

I imagine that Fritz is watching the clouds as well. I think of Fatty Dienst—remember him?—and how he must be sitting right now in the German trench looking at those same clouds. I imagine that _he_ sees sausages and mounds of greasy minced beef. But maybe not. I wonder if he thinks of London as much as I do, if he thinks about his little shop and how you used to go to see him. Remember how he made you laugh? I don't understand how we could end up fighting against each other, but there it is. The gods must be cruel, as they say.

Well, there I go again. I'm sorry, Johnny. You must think I'm a miserable old geezer, always complaining about this or that. But in truth it's not so bad, not nearly as awful as I've been making it out.

Believe it or not, a billiards table came yesterday. We had a little tournament down in the dugout, a little singsong afterwards. Why, it's almost like a holiday.

I'm as healthy as ever, and very well fed. There's not a day that I don't tuck in to a tin of plum-and-apple jam. And I'm among the finest lot of lads I could ever hope to find.

So I shan't trouble you anymore with stories of shells and bullets and things. It's enough to tell you that I'm healthy and happy, and thinking of you always.

Enclosed is one little soldier. Nothing special about him.

   All my love,
   Dad

I was almost scared to see the new soldier. I held it, feeling through the paper, trying to guess what it looked like.

"Well?" said Auntie Ivy. "You'd better open it."

I wanted to wait. There was another letter from my mother, and I asked to hear it first. I closed my eyes.

I hope to come to see you soon. I can't make any promises, but I'll do my very best.

"There!" said Auntie Ivy. "That should put a smile on your face."

I wish I could spend a week or more, and take you away at the end. But the arsenal is bursting at the seams. The work goes on round the clock. The best I'll be able to do is spend a night with you and your aunt. Oh, Johnny, it's so very long ago that I sent you off to Cliffe. I certainly never dreamed that so much time would pass before I saw you again. We told each other that the war would be over by Christmas, and we'd be together then. We never thought that Christmas might not come. But if I'm not with you, and if the two of us aren't with your father, it certainly won't be Christmas.

"She says she loves you, of course," said Auntie Ivy. "Now open your soldier, Johnny."

Auntie squinted through her glasses as I tore away the paper. She looked like someone pulling a Christmas cracker, expecting a fright when it banged. Then I pulled the soldier out, and she smiled. "Now that's better. That's the sort of thing I expect to see from your father." She laughed. "Playing billiards, indeed."

Stiff and chunky, bright with paint, he was more toy-like than the others, something close to my nutcracker men, my very first soldiers. He held his rifle at his side, and he grinned a real grin—a beaming smile. It was a tiny rifle that he carried, so I knew right away what my father had sent: a model of his happier self to replace the gloomy one he'd made before. But this little figure wore a scarf tied above his service cap, the ends sticking up like a rabbit's ears.

I thought it was rather silly, but I was so, so pleased to see it. Auntie Ivy clapped her hands and laughed.

"You'll have to show that one to Mr. Tuttle," she said. "He would like to come and see it, I think."

But I was too busy to go and see him on a day that I didn't have to. School had finished for the holidays, and I spent every moment in the garden. From breakfast to lunch, from tea until supper, I battled with my soldiers. In rain and cold I crouched there, hoping it was really true that whatever happened in the garden would happen again in France. If there was the slightest chance of that—if there was any hope at all—the war might end by Christmas, and my father might come home. From dawn until dusk I bombarded my nutcracker men, until the ground all around them was broken and torn. Then I ran my Frenchmen up against them, over and over, again and again. My little wooden dad, his bandages off and his wounds healed, watched the war from his trench. The British never attacked; only the Frenchmen. And they slaughtered the nutcracker soldiers.

Sarah was gone. Her mother had taken her north to Suffolk, to the little town of Bury St. Edmunds. They had left on the last day of the school term, and Sarah hadn't said goodbye.

The sergeant I didn't see until a week before Christmas.

It was the nineteenth day of December, a Saturday. Neither I nor Mr. Tuttle had talked of ending our lessons, but they were winding down. Distressed that no boy had come forward to admit to hurting his roses, Mr. Tuttle was only waiting for Christmas to submit his resignation. And I was still too ashamed to tell him the truth.

That afternoon, I got a shock to see him packing his belongings. He had half a dozen tea chests in his front room, and was filling them with his little trinkets. One whole wall was bare, except for the picture of his wife.

"Are you really leaving?" I asked.

"I am," he said. "If nothing changes."

"Because of your roses?"

"Because of the principle," he said. "I've set a course and I have to follow it. That's the measure of a man, after all: to see things through no matter how distasteful, no matter what others think."

"But what will happen to your roses?" I asked.

"They'll grow wild, I suppose," said Mr. Tuttle. "I'll take a cutting, of course, and try to start over somewhere else. But the rest?" He was packing his figurines, rolling each one into a white cloth. "If they survive the winter they should do quite well. They'll spread from my garden into the fields, from the fields to the forests, all across Kent."

"Like an army," I said.

"Yes. A beautiful, red-coated army."

From there we slipped into our lesson, the army of roses becoming armies of men. Mr. Tuttle distressed me by talking of wars that went on for years and years.

There were some, he said, that went on so long that they were ended by the grandchildren of the men that started them. "Imagine that," he said. "Your father comes home an old man. You grow up and go off to the war, and then you come home and have children. And years from now your children grow up and go to fight in the same trenches as you and your father."

"It couldn't happen," I said. But I remembered the Highlander who had carried me up to the train. He had told me the same thing; he had told me that my dad would never come home. "No, it couldn't happen," I said again, fiercely.

"Oh, but it's happened before," Mr. Tuttle told me. "There's wars that lasted a hundred years."

We reached the end of the *Iliad* that day. Mighty Achilles killed poor Hector, the Trojan prince, and dragged his body around and around the city walls. He dragged it all over the place, until it was smashed and broken. But the gods made it whole again, and the king of Troy had to go and beg for it back from the Greeks. There was a funeral that seemed to go on forever, with races and games, and people talking about Hector. Outside the walls, the Greeks were getting ready to attack again.

Mr. Tuttle wiped away tears, but I thought it was a silly ending.

"Is that all?" I asked.

"What more could there be?" said Mr. Tuttle. "It's prophetic, Johnny. Wars might pause, but they'll never stop. And if heroes can be killed, what's the use for bravery except to be mourned and remembered?"

I left his house rather sadder than when I'd started

out. And with every step through the gloom and the mud, I became a little more disheartened.

Mr. Tuttle, who dreaded the cold for the sake of his roses, was glad for the steady, endless rain. But I hated it. I was homesick and lonely, longing for my mother to come and take me to London again. I couldn't see how my dad would ever get home in time.

And now the days were so short that I had to hurry along the footpaths. Through thickets and stands of trees, the darkness seemed to chase me. It came like a rising river, filling the hollows. It covered the ruined cottage and flowed through the woods, all the shadows gathering there. It flooded the little cemetery to the very tops of the gravestones. A bat flitted across them, its wings whistling as it hunted for mice.

I passed the field quickly, then came to the forest again, so dark that I was scared to go in it. I veered from the path, down the edge of old Storey's farm. I trampled through the mud, and stumbled over hummocks I couldn't see. And I nearly shouted with fright when I heard the rustle in the trees.

Branches snapped. Something howled in the darkness. Then the orange cat came streaking from the forest. It banged against my legs, hissed and darted off. In an instant it was gone, but I would have liked to chase it, to kick it if I could. I was angry it had scared me, until I heard something coming behind it.

I stared at the trees, too frightened to run. I saw something moving in there, coming straight toward me. Then it turned aside, and slid along in its snap and crash of branches. I dropped to the ground, and out from the woods came the sergeant.

He passed close enough that I could hear him groan as he breathed. There was a bruise on his face, an ugly blotch like a slab of raw liver. His uniform was all in tatters, his trouser leg split open to his knee. Around his leg was a filthy bandage, stained with dirt and blood. I could smell the rot below it, the same sour stench that had leaked from the windows of Fatty Dienst's boarded-up shop.

He staggered on across the field, hunched like a gnome. He went in lurches and hops, his bandaged leg as stiff as a piece of wood. He was the dog-faced soldier my father had made, a weary and horrid thing that groped along, that sometimes crawled where the ground was rough and broken. He stopped, and moaned, then started again. He went on through the rain and the mud—through the gathering darkness—to the little cemetery where the grave markers stood like stepping-stones in the river of shadows.

He crossed the fence and dropped behind it. I saw him lurch across the mound of a grave and pass behind a marble cross. And he vanished then, in the gloom of rain and blackness, as though he sank within the soil.

I turned and ran, reeling from humps to hollows, from grass to mud to thorns. I staggered around logs, around old, fallen fences, and—at last—hurtled down through a ditch and up to the road. Then I stopped for a moment, but not any longer. From the north, toward Cliffe, came a clang of metal, like a tin bell tolling, and a glimmer of light flashed on the road. And around a bend appeared old Storey Sims.

He came weaving toward me, from side to side, from ditch to ditch. I saw the lantern in his outstretched hook, its flickering light shining only on the front of him, on his arm and chest and face. That seemed to be all there was of Storey Sims, just an image of a man shining in the rain, just half a man—without any legs—floating along on the shadow river.

I was even more scared of old Storey than I was of the sergeant. I raced toward home, splashing through puddles. Each time I looked back the lantern was there, chasing me down the long and empty road.

"Don't slam the door," Auntie told me as I barreled inside.

She was still at her knitting, her silvery head lowered toward it. The big balls of yarn had shrunk to the size of walnuts. Her needles ticked and tapped as steadily as watches.

"How's Mr. Tuttle?" she asked.

The house calmed me. It soothed me with its warmth and smells.

"Well?" she said. She looked up at me, and *tsk*ed and shook her head. "How can a boy make such a mess of himself just walking from house to house?"

I was filthy and wet. Blades of yellow grass were plastered round my ankles; I wore bracelets of thorns. I said, "I ran all the way home. I saw the sergeant again."

"Where?" she asked. But I didn't get a chance to tell her, because someone came and pounded on the door. It shook the wood and boomed through the house, a sound as loud as thunder but steady as Auntie's needles.

"Well, don't just stand there gawking," she said. "Go and see who it is."

The door seemed to bulge toward me; its hinges rattled with each pounding of fists. I turned the latch and it flew open, and there on the step was old Storey Sims. His boots were huge and hobnailed, his clothes all rough and patched. He had tangled hair and a beard like a thatch of black grass. His hook was raised, ready to hammer again, and I cringed away from him. Then he lifted the lantern and it blinded my eyes.

"You were out on the road," he shouted. "Did you see anyone else? Did you see a young man?"

I didn't see his hook coming out from the glare. It took hold of my shoulder, and he shook me. "Answer!" shouted Storey.

"Let him go!" said Auntie Ivy, rising from her chair. "You crazy old man, let him go."

But he only held me harder. He leaned forward, and his face swooped down to mine, shining in the lantern. "Answer me!" he shouted again.

"You don't give him a chance," said Auntie Ivy. She thumped up behind me and pulled me back from the door. "How dare you come here in the dead of night and frighten the wits from the boy?"

"Good God, woman!" roared Storey Sims. His lantern hung above all of us, smelling of kerosene. "Murdoch's my son. What would you have me do?"

"Not scaring young boys half to death," she said. "Now, stop this nonsense. Come in from the rain like a civilized man."

Auntie Ivy could have kept a mad bull from charging by telling it to "stop this nonsense." Old Storey Sims lowered his lantern and let his shoulders droop. He turned in a moment from anger to sadness.

"I won't come in," he said. "Murdoch's out in the rain, and I have to keep looking. I have to keep searching."

"Leave it be," said Auntie, as gently as she could. "If Murdoch was out there, don't you think he'd know where to find you?"

"And what if he can't?" asked Storey. "What if he's lost? How can I rest thinking he's there?"

Auntie hugged my shoulders. Old Storey Sims glared at me, then touched his forehead and said, "Good night to you, Ivy." He went down to the path, out through the gate, with his lantern clanging at the end of his arm.

Auntie Ivy closed the door. She looked down at me. "Johnny?" she said. "Did you really see your sergeant tonight?"

I nodded.

"Do you still think he's Murdoch?"

"I don't know," I said. "He gave me his tag, and it said his name is Thomas Cade. But he *looks* like Murdoch, Auntie."

"Where did he go?"

"He came out of the woods," I said. "And he vanished in the cemetery."

"Gracious." She sighed. "Johnny, that's where every Sims is buried."

CHAPTER 16

December 18, 1914

Dearest Johnny,

Guess who sent me a present? Princess Mary! She gave me the nicest little tin box, full of fine cigars and a special box of matches. I knew she wouldn't forget your old dad, and the hobbyhorse I made her years ago.

Really, Johnny, she sent something to everyone. We were all quite pleased, and it was only the start of it. There are so many packages coming to the front that the trains are running late! Besides the wonderful socks I've got a plum pudding from The Times, *a bottle of Horlicks tablets from Mrs. Brown downstairs, a fountain pen from that geezer who had the shop next to mine. People I've never heard of and will surely never meet are sending little gifts to the whole battalion, and we're outfitted now in fine form, in balaclavas and socks and furry coats.*

Now don't you dare tell this to your mother, but I rather envy the single men. They are getting heaps and heaps of things that come addressed to "A Lonely Soldier." It's all quite overwhelming. My section of the trench looks like a stall in Petticoat Lane!

Everyone is thinking very strongly of home. For many of the lads this is the first Christmas they have ever spent away from their families, and I have seen them sniffing the wrappings of their little presents, trying to catch the smells of England, of women, of home. I have seen some break into tears at the sight of a packet of matches. And in the clouds now we're seeing tinsel and garlands and evergreen boughs.

Across the way, the Hun is planning his own sort of celebration. Every night we hear the tramp of boots on his duckboards, great numbers of men marching up to the front. Word has it he's readying a big offensive for Christmas Day, hoping to catch us off our guard. Well, he's in for a nasty surprise, I'm afraid, for that is just the sort of thing we expect from that lot of unholy barbarians. Christmas or not, we'll be open for business. And we'll be sending lots and lots of nine-pound presents his way that morning.

Auntie Ivy closed her eyes. "No," she whispered. "Not on Christmas Day." Little tears dribbled onto her cheeks. "They can't attack on Christmas Day."

"I hope they do," I said.

Her eyes snapped open. "You hope for no such thing."

"I do," I said. Christmas was only five days off.

"You foolish child."

"But, Auntie, the side that attacks always comes out the worst." It was what the sergeant had told me, and Sarah too. "We have to get the Huns out of their trenches. We have to catch them in the open and—"

"Stop it!" she shouted. "You bloodthirsty boy." She slapped me on the cheek.

It shocked me more than it hurt. It shocked me into tears. "Why did you do that?" I cried.

She threw my dad's letter onto the table, and went swishing from the room. She hadn't even read right through it, and I shouted at her: "Come and finish the letter!"

"You don't deserve to hear it," she said.

I hated her then. I wished she was in France, squishing through the mud in her huge black shoes. I hoped a sniper could see her silver hair bobbing down the trench.

"I want to know what he sent me," I shouted.

"Then open it, Johnny," she said.

I cursed her under my breath. I called her a wicked old witch, and pulled away paper. I called her a fool and a hag, and pulled away more. And out from the wrappings came an aeroplane.

It wasn't my favorite toy, but it was close. It was my third favorite thing. Six inches long, graceful and lovely, it had a little propeller that spun when I tapped it. Black crosses were painted on the wings, and in the cockpit sat a nutcracker man, only his head showing, his big teeth grinning. I flew the aeroplane across the table, with a sound of engines purring on my lips: "Brrrrrrr."

I flew it from the kitchen, running underneath it as it dipped and soared to the hall. Then it landed there, and waited as I put on my boots and my macintosh.

"Contact!" said the pilot. I spun the propeller. "Brrrr. Brrrr."

The aeroplane did a wingover through the door. It swooped down the steps and soared across the garden. The pilot was looking down, scouting the front for the big Christmas push.

I armed him with a dirt bomb, and he flew above the front. "I will try to hit their cheneral."

But I was scared to drop bombs on the British. So the pilot missed, and his glob of dirt fell miles and miles behind the lines. Then he flew home, and I crouched in the mud to plan the Christmas attack.

General Cedric hopped forward. "Strengthen the trenches!" he shouted. "I think the Huns are coming."

All that day I worked on my trenches. I fetched more butcher's string and doubled my coils of barbed wire. I kept thinking how the church bells would ring when Auntie Ivy's garden lay covered with all my nutcracker men. I would wipe them out in one huge attack, in a single rush on Christmas morning. My little wooden father would be right at the center; he would kill half of them himself, and my real dad would come home a week later, with medals all over his chest.

The orange cat went slinking past that afternoon, along the top of the wall. Thin as sticks, its fur matted, it sat at the corner where the sergeant had stood. It howled at me, but whenever I moved it darted away.

"Go on to Mr. Tuttle's," I told it. "He'll give you cream." Then it howled again, in such a sad voice that I couldn't bear to listen. So I chased it off with dirt bombs, and went back to planning my war.

The rain turned to hail. It sizzled through the branches above me, slashing down on my shoulders, on the back of my head, as I crouched over my wooden army. It filled the cracks among the stones of the wall, and it covered the ground with tiny pellets that sparkled and shone. And I kept moving the nutcracker men into their trenches, packing them shoulder to shoulder.

Then the gray sunlight faded, and the ground began to freeze. The British soldiers glittered under frosty coats, and I couldn't bend my fingers anymore. They clamped like claws to my nutcracker men. And when Auntie Ivy called me in, I stood up and left my shadow behind me. All the garden was white except for that spot where I'd crouched at the trenches, where the hail hadn't fallen.

"Why, you're frozen stiff," said Auntie Ivy. "I forgot you were there, you poor thing."

I had a bath—she made me do it—and sat in a swirl of steam as the ice melted from my hair. My teeth chattered; I shivered as each bit of sleet trickled down my back. Then I put on pajamas and huddled by the stove, wrapped in a huge towel, as Auntie Ivy brought me cocoa so thick that it stuck to my teeth.

"Oh, Johnny," she said. "Why didn't you come in and get warm?"

"I didn't think of it," I said.

"You could have caught your death out there."

She felt my forehead, then banked up the fire. The kitchen grew sweltering hot. And she kept looking at me sideways. "Do you want to hear the last bit of it now?"

"Of what?" I asked.

"Your father's letter, of course."

I sniffed. "Yes, please."

She sat in the squeaky old rocking chair and put on her spectacles. The letter crinkled as she unfolded it. In a mumbly voice, she read very quickly down to the place where she had stopped.

I tightened the towel around my bare feet.

This morning an aeroplane flew across our bit of sky. It passed at too great a height for me to tell if it was one of ours or one of theirs. But it flew to the west, toward the German lines, and it crossed our slit of clouds so fast that I could scarcely believe it. Why, it traveled in seconds farther than I've gone since I came to the front, farther than I might ever go until the war is over. And how I wished I was on it.

I would let it whisk me to Kent, to land on the road that passes your house. And I would be there sooner than I could, by walking, even pass beyond the sound of the guns. And then you'd jump in and we'd fly on to London, right to Regent's Park. And we'd spend Christmas together, you and me and your mother.

I'll be lonely without you, Johnny. I have to admit it. But I'm sure your Auntie Ivy is looking after you well enough. Have you put up the tree? It's been years and years since I've seen it, but I remember it as a rather splendid tree. There was lots of room underneath for all the presents and the packages.

Will you have a goose this year? Will you have a slice for me?

Enclosed, one little aeroplane. And only a bit of my love, I'm afraid. No parcel in the world would be big enough to hold all of that.

Dad

"Where's the tree?" I asked.

Auntie Ivy took off her little spectacles. "I don't know," she said.

"Maybe it's in the storeroom."

"Maybe so," she said. "But I'm not sure we should put it up."

"Why not?" I asked.

"I don't think you'd like it," she said.

But nothing would do then except that I would see that tree standing in the parlor. I pestered Auntie Ivy until she caved in and said, "Oh, all right!" So up we went.

She knew right where it was, in a box inside another. The picture on the lid was faded and torn, but it showed a whole family sitting below a monstrous tree that sparkled with candles.

"It *is* splendid," I said.

"Well, that's not quite how it looks," said Auntie Ivy. "It's not so grand as your father remembers."

We took the box down to the parlor, and my heart fell the moment that we opened it. There was a stick for a trunk, and bent wires for branches. Tiny glass ornaments rattled around in the bottom, along with half a dozen candles in little tin cups.

"Our father—your grandfather—bought this one year," said Auntie Ivy. "He set it up on Christmas Eve, and we saw it in the morning. The candles were burning. And your father—he wasn't much older than you—thought it was the most magical thing he had ever seen."

The trunk was only two feet long. It fitted into a little wooden tub painted the dull red of old bricks.

"The bristles are made of goose feathers," said Auntie. "You'll see how it goes."

We wedged the trunk into the tub, then stuck the branches on. They fanned out like spokes, in four layers growing smaller toward the top. The needles didn't look like feathers, or much like needles either. There were funny bunches of red berries at the tip of each branch, and the whole tree looked spindly and short.

"Your grandfather would set it on a stool," said Auntie Ivy. "I suppose your dad's forgotten that, and remembers a tree that towered above him."

"But wouldn't he know from later?" I asked.

"We only used it for two Christmases," said Auntie Ivy. "Then your grandfather went off to that awful war in Siam, and he never came home from that."

I picked the glass ornaments from the box. Auntie Ivy sorted through the candleholders.

"Does Mr. Tuttle have a tree?" she asked.

"No," I said. "He'll be leaving soon, I think."

"Leaving?" Her face fell. "Why on earth is he leaving?"

It amazed me that there was some local news she didn't know. I said, "His roses got damaged."

"And he's leaving for that?"

"Because no one owned up," I said.

She looked terribly sad, as though her world had ended. "I know they mean everything to him," she said. "His wife's roses; she started them. He kept them going as though they were children she left him. But he can't go away."

"He's already packing," I said. "You know all those things in his house?"

"No," said Auntie. "I haven't been to his house since his wife died."

"But he lives just down the road."

"And keeps himself to himself," said Auntie. "Remember that day he came here, because you weren't in school? That was the first time in seven years. He's lived like a hermit, nearly. But you were changing him; you were bringing him out of his shell."

The tree shook as I put the last ornaments on. Auntie

Ivy held on to the tub. She said, "I think you should invite him for Christmas dinner."

"All right." We started fitting the candles in their little tin cups. "He can celebrate the end of the war."

"Oh, that could be years away, Johnny," she said.

"No, Auntie." I clipped the candles on the tree. "The war's going to end on Christmas."

"They used to say that, Johnny," she said, staring at me through the wiry branches. "But not anymore. It might go on—"

"Yes it is," I told her. "It's going to stop on Christmas Day."

"And how do you know that?" she said.

"I just know."

"This isn't to do with your soldiers, is it?" She frowned when I nodded. "For heaven's sake, we've been over that. Wooden soldiers can't decide the war."

"I don't know," I said. "I think they might at Christmas."

She sighed. "Do you know what this is sounding like?"

"It's not rubbish," I said.

"It's mindless chatter," she told me. "I can't *abide* mindless chatter."

At the bottom of the box I found a little Father Christmas with his flowing beard and long red dressing gown. There was a spot for him on the very tip of the trunk, and I stood him there as the tree swayed and shook.

"Well, it's not so bad," said Auntie Ivy. She touched the branches the way Mr. Tuttle had touched his roses. "It's a brave little tree, I suppose."

"It *is* going to look splendid," I said.

"Oh, Johnny," she said. "Won't you please go and ask Mr. Tuttle?"

"I think I'll take him a present," I said.

She beamed. "That's very kind of you."

I let her think what she wanted, but it really wasn't kindness. If I gave a present to someone, I thought, he would have to give one back to me.

I took the money that was left over from Guy Fawkes Day and bought a box of Bovril for my father, and a little rosebush for Mr. Tuttle. It was just a withered stump with a single twig, but the shopkeeper told me it would grow into a very fine rose.

Mr. Tuttle nearly cried when he saw it. He held it like a baby, in both his hands. He said, "I don't think I've ever been given something that means so much to me."

"Is it as good as your old ones?" I asked.

He looked at the stump, at the tiny arm branching from it, and I could see that he was trying to find something to say that wouldn't disappoint me. He was too honest to lie, but too kind to say no. Finally he smiled and told me, "I shall treasure it even more."

"You won't have to move away now, will you?" I asked.

"Oh, I don't know," he sighed. "We'll see."

"I'm sorry it's not a bit bigger," I said.

"It will grow, Johnny. Don't worry about that," said Mr. Tuttle. "In a few years it will be as big as Glory. The flowers will be just as pretty as hers."

I thought he was joking, but he wasn't. "You give your roses names?" I asked.

"The new ones, yes," he said. "You see, Johnny, Glory wasn't just any rose." He cradled my little stump and added, in a hurry, "Not that this one is. But Glory was a hybrid, a brand-new thing."

He took me into his house. There were more tea chests in his front room, a stack of them against the wall he'd bared. His black gown, neatly folded, lay on top of the pile. We went through to the kitchen and sat at a table where all his silverware had been arranged in tidy patterns.

"A rose grower does the work of God," said Mr. Tuttle. "I was *creating* something, Johnny. In the spring Glory was going to bloom for the first time, and the world would have something new and beautiful. In the midst of a war, the world would be a little better for what I was doing in my garden."

He made me feel dreadful, all rotten inside. I wondered what he would say if I told him that I was the one who had killed his Glory rose.

He was touching the stump I'd given him, peeling bits of bark from its frail little branch, already starting it going. "Whoever harmed Glory harmed the whole world," he said. "But myself most of all. My wife bred the parents and I was breeding the child. My wife lived on in those roses."

I was trying to decide how to tell him the truth when his mood turned suddenly to anger. "And he never came forward! That cowardly boy," he said. "If he came to me now I would thrash him for what he has done."

My shame and my fear must have shown on my face. Mr. Tuttle softened his voice, and even smiled. "I'm sorry," he said. "Here you are, the only one who has stood by me, the bearer of this wonderful gift, and I'm venting all my anger on you, the one who least deserves it."

I hung my head.

"You restore my faith in boys," he told me. "You've been so kind, you and your aunt."

"I wish you wouldn't leave," I said.

"Bless you, Johnny. Perhaps I shouldn't."

"We hoped you would come for Christmas dinner," I said. "Auntie sent me to ask you."

That seemed to please him greatly. "I would love to come," he said.

CHAPTER 17

December 21, 1914

Dearest Johnny,
 Your box of Bovril arrived today, and let me tell you that it caused quite a stir among my mates. I brewed up a cup straight away, and I wish you could have seen their faces. Green with envy? Why, that doesn't begin to describe it.
 We had a lantern show last night and a billiards match this morning. It's such a pleasant change from the way the war used to be that I'm almost ashamed to tell you about it. In fact I can't think of much more to add, so this will be a rather short letter.
 Thank you so much for your gift. I hope you're not angry that I didn't wait until Christmas to open it.
 I've not had time to make you a soldier, what with the football and cricket and everything. Please forgive me, Johnny. I love you so much.
 Have to go now.
   All my love,
   Dad

Dad sent the letter in the same sort of green envelope that had arrived just before the victory. Auntie Ivy put it away in her wooden box, and I trudged back to Cliffe, to buy presents for Auntie and Mum.

It was a cold morning, the gray clouds bulging with rain or maybe snow. I wore my overcoat, and went north up the road to the village. The few coins I had jingled in my pocket.

It was easy to shop for Auntie. I bought her a pair of knitting needles, thinking her old ones would soon be worn away by all their clicking and scraping. But I couldn't decide what to get for my mum.

I went all through the shops, then around them again. I went from one to the other, looking at ribbons and hat pins and writing paper. I looked at candles and tapers and tiny horses meant to dangle from bracelets. But the things that I liked were too dear, and I went back to the first shop and started again.

The geezer who'd sold me fireworks asked what I was looking for.

"Something for my mum," I said.

"Ah. Perhaps she'd like one of these."

He put them out on the counter, fancy little boxes full of fancy little chocolates. There were some like tiny eggs and some like seashells. They all looked very expensive. Right away I knew that my mum would love them. "How much do they cost?" I asked.

"Oh, they vary," said the geezer. "How much do you have?"

I took out all my coins: three pennies, a ha'penny and a farthing. I turned my pockets inside out, but there wasn't more than that.

"It's all I have," I said. "My dad's at the front and my mum's in Woolwich, and my auntie's a skinflint, sir."

His fingers came down on my pennies. He nudged them toward me, then hooked them around and slid them into his palm. "I'll go to the poorhouse," he said. "But you're close enough. There's even a farthing left over to buy yourself a sweetie."

I pushed the chocolates into my pocket and started for home. It was already late afternoon, but if I hurried down the footpaths I could still get there before the twilight brought old Storey Sims out with his lantern and his hook.

The light had no shadows, and the forest seemed thick and gloomy. I ran down the path, hurdling roots and frozen puddles, my elbows brushing on crackly bushes. I pretended that my knitting needles were swords, and I slashed them at the twigs. I was a hussar, charging, and the sound of my feet echoed from the trees like the hooves of horses. I kept running, past the orchard, past the crumbled cottage.

And a voice cried out: a howl.

It was an eerie sound that made me stop and stand absolutely still. I wasn't sure just where the voice had come from.

I heard it again, and turned toward it. The ruined heap of a stone wall loomed above the bushes. The sound had come from there.

It was the orange cat, I thought. I laughed and shook myself, and said, "It's just the cat."

But then it called my name.

"Johnny," it said. "Help me, Johnny."

I didn't move.

"Help me," said the voice.

I saw the sergeant then, his head, his battered cap. I saw him in the gloom among the fallen stones, and his hand came up and beckoned. And he moaned. He moaned such a heartbroken sound that I couldn't pass him by.

I walked toward him, through the dead grass and the leaves the wind had scattered. I reached the stones and put my hands on them—they were cold as ice—and peered down at the sergeant where he lay on his back, on the ground, all twisted in the rubble. His face was white and it glimmered with sweat. His fingers were like white worms writhing on his throat.

"I'm cold," he said. "So cold."

"Then why are you lying here?" I asked.

He closed his eyes and winced and jerked upright with another horrible moan. Clutching at his bandaged leg, his head thrashing from side to side, he panted like a dog before falling back again. Though I shook from the cold, he was sweating. A trickle of sweat dribbled from under his cap, down his forehead. He mopped it away, smearing it across the bruises that had spread to both cheeks.

"I'm dying," he said. "Oh, Johnny, help me."

"How?" I asked.

"Stay with me for a while."

I sat on the stones of the fallen cottage, wishing that Mr. Tuttle was with me, or even Auntie Ivy. I didn't know what to do to help the sergeant, and I didn't want to stay.

"I saw him again," he said. "The angel." His hand shot out and grasped at his leg. The pain took all the breath from him, and for a minute he couldn't speak at all. Then again he said, "I'm so cold."

I took off my coat and covered him with it, or only his chest; my coat was so small. As I bent over him I smelled the rot in his flesh, and what I thought was the mud of the trenches still caked on his boots and his clothes.

The sergeant opened his eyes. They were huge, all yellow and dull. "There he is," he said. "Do you see him, Johnny? Do you see how he glows?"

I looked behind me. There was nothing there but a pale smudge of sunlight, an orange smear on the clouds.

"He's coming now," said the sergeant.

He made me so scared that I couldn't bear to sit there anymore. "I'll bring some help," I said. But when I tried to leave, his hand clenched on my boot.

"No," he said. "Just stay with me. Talk to me."

"About what?"

"Anything. The war; your father. Tell me about James."

"It's not so bad anymore," I said. "My dad's playing billiards in the dugout. He went to a picture show."

I heard a bubbling in his chest, a wheeze that came out from his throat. It took me a moment to realize that the sergeant was laughing.

"Is that what he told you?" he asked.

"Yes," I said.

"Poor James. What a good soul. He wouldn't want you to worry."

"It's true," I said.

"No, Johnny, it's not. There's no billiards, no picture shows. It's mud and more mud, death and more death."

The sergeant groaned. "It will never change and it will never stop. The guns, the shells, the rats and the mud."

"It's not like that anymore," I said.

"It will always be that way. It will never stop," he said. "The battles go on and on. The dead pile up in no-man's-land. The shells bury them and unearth them again."

"Stop it!" I said. "My dad never lies."

"Believe what you like." He trembled with a sudden pain. "It's a horror, is what it is. I saw the trench collapse, and a dead man's hand appear, reaching from the mud. I saw a soldier hang his canteen on the hooks of those fingers. And I should be there, Johnny. It's where I belong."

"You were wounded," I said. "You're a hero."

He shook his head, but it only lolled from side to side. "I'm not that."

There was a haunted look in his eyes. I was glad when he closed them.

His face had shrunk to his skull. But it was the same face in the picture at Storey's farm.

"Murdoch?" I whispered.

His eyes flickered, but didn't open. "You know," he said. "Do others know? Does my father know?"

"He goes looking for you," I said.

"Don't tell him you've seen me." A tremble started in his hand and shook up through his arm.

"Why won't you go home?" I asked.

"He wouldn't understand. I did it myself, Johnny."

"Did what?"

"I shot myself." Sweat beaded up on his face. "I couldn't bear it anymore. The misery; the fear. I'm a coward, not a hero."

"But you still need help," I said.

Even his breath made him shake. "My dad was a soldier; his dad too. He would hate me for this."

"I won't tell him," I promised. "Only my auntie."

"No one can know." He winked, and it was ghastly to see. "It's our secret, Johnny. Yours and mine."

"And Thomas Cade's," I said.

"No," said Murdoch. "He was on the hospital ship, coming home." He moved his shoulders, fitting down among the stones. "The doctors already knew what I'd done, I think. I saw them whispering, pointing at me. When the ship docked I'd be arrested, then shot for desertion. That night Thomas died. I changed my tag with his; I put some of my things in his pockets."

He started to shake more violently. I tightened my coat around his shoulders, but it didn't seem to help him. His leg twisted, and he moaned, but his eyes stayed closed. "Do you have any food?" he asked.

"No," I said. But I did. Mum's chocolates were in my coat pocket, inches from his hand. My money was gone; they were all I could buy her.

Murdoch sighed. His breath rattled. "When I'm gone, cover me over," he said. "Some dirt, some stones. I don't want the dogs to get me."

"Please don't talk like that," I said. "I can bring you help. They can make you better."

"For what?" he asked. "To shoot me? To send me back? I'd rather die here than go back."

His arm groped under my coat. His white fingers came out from the edge, curled like the hooks he'd seen in the trenches. "Say you'll do it," he said. "Just cover me over," he said. "But make sure that I'm gone."

I couldn't do that, and I didn't want him to die. I took

out my chocolates and fed them to him. He gobbled them down.

Right away he was calm, and he lay on the stones with a peaceful look on his face. "I didn't think I would ever eat chocolate again," he said. "God bless you, Johnny."

I held his hand, but I hated him for what he was asking.

Murdoch lay quietly, his chest hardly lifting. Now and then a tremor came through his hand into mine. Then his eyes opened again. They started as slits, then widened suddenly into huge, horrid balls. "There he is now," he said. "The angel. He's here."

His head eased back, and he fell into an awful sleep that made him twitch and cry. I imagined that he was dreaming himself back to the war, though what he was seeing I couldn't even guess. Then his hand flew up to ward something off, and he howled. And I thought that he wasn't asleep at all, that he wasn't dreaming, and whatever he saw was really *there*. A man, a beast, an angel—whatever it was—it was oozing with the shadows into the ruins of the cottage. And it made me shake with fright.

I ran from that place. I scrambled over the stones, down to the grass and leaves, and I raced along the footpath, back to Auntie Ivy's.

I climbed over the wall, and I saw my nutcracker men in their black slits of trenches, their gnashing teeth in a ghostly line. I ran into the house, shouting for Auntie.

She was holding a telegram.

"It's for you," she said.

I could hardly speak. "My dad?" I whispered.

"No," she said. "It's your mother."

"My mother?" I asked. "What happened?"

"Oh, don't be silly," she said. "Nothing has *happened*. She sent you a wire to say that she won't be coming for Christmas."

I started to cry. On top of everything else, of Murdoch and the secret I'd made, this seemed like the end of the world. "She was going to take me home," I blubbered. "She promised to come and get me."

"Well, she's not doing it to spite you," said Auntie. "With all the suffering in the world, I don't think it's a tragedy that you won't see your mother at Christmas."

"But why?" I asked.

"Why do you think? The war, Johnny. The—" She stopped. "Where's your coat?"

I was almost surprised to find it missing. I'd run so fast and so far that I was hot even without it.

"Well?" she said. "Where is it?"

I couldn't tell her the truth. "I didn't have it with me," I said.

"You *did*," she snapped. "I saw you put it on."

"Then I must have lost it," I said.

She gave me a suspicious look. "Well, you'd better go and find it. First thing in the morning, young man."

I didn't know what to do or what to tell her. The night turned cold and the snow started falling. I thought of Murdoch shivering in his ruins, but I didn't tell Auntie. I let him lie there all that night and into the morning of Christmas Eve.

Chapter 18

December 22, 1914

Dearest Johnny,

Are you having a white Christmas? We're having a rather muddy one here, I'm afraid. It's made a proper mess of our horseshoe pitch, let me tell you that. And we've fairly given up on the footraces altogether.

Right now I'm leaning back in the dugout, and there's a pot of tea on the go beside me, brewing away on my little billy-can stove. I'm waiting my turn at billiards, and then I think I might wander over to the picture show, if I make it past the campfire, that is. Some of the lads have planned a caroling, and I understand that there's going to be eggnog for all. And pudding, of course, though I'm frightened it won't be as good as your mother's.

Do you remember the one she made last year? It was enormous, wasn't it? You said, "It's big as a tram." Then you put all your little soldiers sitting on top for the ride from the kitchen to the table. Do you remember that, how you walked ahead clanging like a bell?

I keep thinking of things like that, the little pleasures of Christmases past. We all do, all the lads. We sit staring at

❖ 170

nothing, seeing our families and our friends, our homes all bright and warm. I keep seeing your mother and yourself, and sometimes it all seems so real that my heart breaks when the picture dissolves.

I'm afraid I must hurry with this. It's almost my turn at billiards now.

The Huns, of course, are making their own preparations. Over there, across no-man's-land, it's march, march, march all night long. Their boots thunder on the boardwalks loud enough to drown out the gramophone. But it turns out I spoke too quickly about Fritz attacking on Christmas. It seems there is nothing to fear in his boxes. Just as we're getting presents from home, so is the Hun, so don't worry about me at Christmas, Johnny.

What do you think Fatty Dienst will get, wherever he is? A pair of socks, perhaps? And he'll think they're special mittens without any thumbs. Poor Fatty; I hope he's well.

That's all the news. Except I have to say that you would laugh to see me now. We look like an army of Cossacks in our wooly hats and thick gloves and furry coats. At least we're warm for most of the time, though I'm afraid it's the coldest Christmas I've ever seen.

Enclosed, one soldier dressed in the latest fashion. It's the best I can do for Christmas, I'm afraid. Next year, God willing, I'll make it up to you, Johnny.

All my love, forever and ever,
Dad

"What a funny soldier," said Auntie as I stripped the wrappings from the figure. "He looks like a ragpicker, Johnny."

There was a floppy hat on his head, a scarf at his neck, enormous boots on his feet. He wore so many clothes that he was round as a snowman, while his cheeks were painted a very bright red.

Auntie Ivy laughed, but I didn't. "What's wrong?" she asked.

"He sounds sort of frightened."

"Your father? He doesn't!"

"He keeps saying, 'I'm afraid,' " I told her.

"That's not what he means." She scowled at the letter, and I saw her lips moving as she read through it again.

To me it was clear; Dad was scared, but didn't want me to know. Like a spy, he had put a secret code into his letter that he had meant only for Auntie to see, but that I had learned by mistake.

"He sounds perfectly fine to me," she said. But now she looked troubled herself.

"But what's in those boxes?" I asked. "What are the Germans bringing up to the front?"

"Presents, of course."

"Maybe mortars," I said.

She took a long breath, then closed her eyes and sighed it out. "Well, if you doubt your own father . . ."

"But he's not telling the truth," I said. "They don't pitch horseshoes. It's not like that at all."

"I suppose you know better," she said.

"I do." I knocked the little soldier on his side. "There's mud everywhere. It falls away and there's bodies inside, their hands reaching out. The soldiers hang their canteens on the—"

"Who's telling you this?" asked Auntie.

"No one." I felt more miserable than I'd ever felt in

my life. I couldn't tell her the truth about anything. At last she stood up, and I thought my troubles were over. But they only got worse.

"Go and find your coat," she said.

The last thing I wanted to do was go and see Murdoch shivering in his old ruin, babbling about angels and things that lurked in the shadows. But Auntie insisted. She even stood over me as I pulled on my Wellingtons.

"Maybe someone else has found it," I said. "Someone who really needs it, Auntie."

"What nonsense," she said. "You're just too lazy to look."

"But what if someone did?" I was sick at the thought of seeing Murdoch. "Should I leave it with him?"

"Johnny," she said, her eyes getting small. "What are you talking about?"

I looked down at my boots so she wouldn't see the tears in my eyes.

"Tell me," she said. "Who could be out there that would need that coat more than you?"

"I don't know," I said. But the words choked in my throat, and came out in only a squeak.

"Who?" she asked again. Then, "Good heavens! Not that soldier?"

Her knees popped as she came down to the floor. "Johnny, where is your coat?"

I hadn't promised not to tell her that. "In the ruins," I said. "But please don't ask me anything else."

"All right," she said calmly. "We'll *both* go out. We'll get to the bottom of this."

We went down the footpath together, in the cold morning of Christmas Eve. Our breaths made puffs of white; our boots creaked on frozen mud, raising flurries from a thin layer of snow. Auntie Ivy, in a red coat and white hat, walked at my side, telling me now to hurry, now to slow down. She wore funny little buttoned boots with sharp toes and chunky heels that skidded on the ground.

"A body could freeze to death out here," said Auntie.

I thought of Murdoch lying among the stones. Would we find him covered in ice, peering up through frozen eyes? Or had his angel come to fetch him, leaving nothing there but my coat?

I took Auntie to the ruin, and she marched straight up through the rubble. In her bright clothes, on the gray and white stones, she looked like a robin at a winter feeder. I went up behind her, my feet cold in my boots, my face tingling with frost. She stumbled and I caught her, and we climbed to the top of the stones.

Below us lay the sergeant, half covered by my coat. His eyes were closed, and his lips had almost no color. Auntie gasped to see him, then hurried down to his side.

"It *is* Murdoch," she whispered. "Oh, Johnny, I'm sorry."

"Is he dead?" I asked.

She bent her face toward his. "He's breathing," she said.

I climbed down beside her as Auntie drew my coat around Murdoch's shoulders. She pulled it up, baring the bandages. "Oh, Johnny," she said. "Look at his leg."

It was crooked between the stones, doubled in size. He had torn big, ragged holes in his bandage, and the flesh underneath was broken and purple, scratched by his nails, oozing a terrible custard.

"Look what they did to him," said Auntie Ivy. "Oh, why is he lying here? Why didn't he go home?"

"He told me he couldn't," I said.

"What else did he tell you?"

"Nothing." I hung my head.

"Johnny, he's dying!" shouted Auntie Ivy.

I couldn't keep my secret. I didn't want to keep it. "He shot himself, Auntie," I said.

"Lord have mercy."

I couldn't look at Murdoch and I couldn't look at Auntie, not with her eyes suddenly full of horror and shock. I looked up at the sky, at the clouds boiling past, through the gap from wall to wall.

"He was scared," I said. "He wanted to get away from the war. But now he's a deserter, and the army will shoot him again if they find him. They'll make him better and shoot him."

"What madness," she cried. "What an awful, horrible war." She dragged her hands down her face, pulling so hard that she stretched all the wrinkles away. Then she took off her gaudy red coat and put it over his legs. "You wait with him, Johnny," she said, standing up.

"Where are you going?" I said.

"To get some help, of course."

"Not Mr. Sims," I said. "Auntie, please; he's not supposed to know."

She was already leaving, scrambling up through the rubble. In a moment she was over the top, clunking down to the path. Her little white hat disappeared.

I heard a quiet rumble underneath my overcoat. I lifted the edge and saw the orange cat curled against Murdoch's chest; it was the cat that had kept him warm.

Then I covered it up, stretched out beside the sergeant, and listened to the purrs. I was still lying there when Auntie Ivy came back, with Mr. Tuttle behind her. He carried his gown, and we worked together to make a litter for Murdoch.

The orange cat stretched, and wandered out, and we carried Murdoch from the ruin, into a drizzle that was already melting the snow. With Mr. Tuttle at his head, Auntie and I at his feet, we carried him along as gently as we could, stopping to rest where the trees gave us shelter. He lay in a murmuring sleep all the way to Mr. Tuttle's house, where we stretched him out on the sofa.

Mr. Tuttle piled logs on the fire. Auntie Ivy took one look at the pile of tea chests—no bigger or smaller than I'd seen it last—and went off to make cocoa for Murdoch. I was put to work tearing bedsheets into bandages; then we all bundled Murdoch in blankets that were fluffy and white. Mr. Tuttle and Auntie sat side by side on the edge of his ottoman, rubbing warmth into the soldier, trying to coax him to drink. Murdoch started shivering—slowly at first—and then so violently that the enormous sofa shook on its wooden legs. Drops of cocoa flew from his lips.

Mr. Tuttle tried to hold him down. "Johnny, go and find Storey," he said.

"What about a doctor?" I asked.

"He's gone to the war, and the nearest one is miles away," said Mr. Tuttle. "We'll send for him too, but first things first. Murdoch must see his father."

"That's not what he wants," I said.

"I suspect he no longer knows what he wants." Mr.

Tuttle pressed his hand on Murdoch's forehead. It was horribly bruised, bright with sweat. "He's got a very high fever, Johnny. He may well have no idea where he is, nor even *who* he is."

"But he knew before," I said. "And he made me *promise* not to tell."

Auntie Ivy put down the cocoa. "We don't have to tell Mr. Sims everything that happened," she said. "We can keep some of it to ourselves."

Mr. Tuttle knew nothing of that. He looked in wonder at my auntie, and then at me. I didn't say a word, but Auntie never kept secrets. "It's self-inflicted," she said, in a whisper.

"Oh, Lord." Mr. Tuttle touched the blankets lumped over the soldier's leg. "He told you this, Johnny?"

"Yes," I said.

"What a weight," he muttered. "What a responsibility to put upon a child." He shook his head and frowned. "Johnny, I'm sorry, but I must side with your aunt. It's the right thing to do."

I was sent away to find old Storey Sims. I was told to bring him back as quickly as I could, to tell him only that Murdoch was there.

It was very cold, and the clouds were such a solid mass that I was sure they stretched all the way to France, that it might be snowing on the battlefield and on the soldiers in their trenches. I thought of my father standing in the cold, with his new wooly clothes all sodden and icy. He wasn't playing billiards or singing songs at a fire; he had never done that. I saw him very clearly, as I trotted up the road. I saw him pounding his hands together, shuffling feet that squelched in the mud, through a rime of crackling ice. I saw the sad, worried look on his face as he waited for Christmas, for the Germans to come.

And then his picture melted away, and I couldn't bring it back. I couldn't even think what he looked like, and it scared me to think I might *never* remember. In the morning there would be a battle, and he might come out of it wounded and shattered. He might not come out of it at all.

I tried to outrun my fears, but they swirled all around me. The Germans bringing up boxes. Dead men's hands. I felt haunted by my fears, as though they battered at my mind. Voices cried at me, one after another. *That* army *of butchers. Zeppelins, Johnny. The Huns came thick as eels. There's wars that last a hundred years.*

The voices chased me to the farm, up the lane to the porch. I kicked and banged at the door.

Old Storey came out, and he glared down at me with the darkest look I'd ever seen.

I said, "Murdoch's—"

"Where?" roared Storey, and I told him.

He didn't wait long enough to get a coat, to even shut the door. He shouted for his wife to come, then bounded from the house and dragged me with him, around the back to a wagon and a harnessed horse. He'd been hauling firewood, and the wagon was half empty now, the ground beside it strewn with short, fat logs.

"Get up!" he shouted, and pitched me onto the wagon's seat. Mrs. Sims came dashing out, and he pitched her up as well. He climbed up with me and shook the reins, and the horse set off at a run.

The wagon swayed and clattered, spilling the wood

from its sides, from its back. The logs tumbled down and bounced along the mud and the grass. I clung to my seat and we dashed along through the clouds of breath the horses made. In moments I was back at Mr. Tuttle's little cottage.

Murdoch still shook on the sofa. The blankets were stained with patches of sweat, with a spot of black blood that had soaked through the new bandages. He seemed only half his size, a trembling lump so unlike the soldier I'd first seen at the wall that I wouldn't have been surprised if old Storey had asked, "Who is this?" But he only said, "Oh, Murdoch. Oh, Murdoch, where have you been?"

Mrs. Sims threw herself down by his head. Old Storey petted and patted at the blankets. "What happened to him?" he asked. "Where did you find him?"

Mr. Tuttle came and stood at my side. "It was Johnny who saved him. Johnny kept him warm."

"But where was he?" asked Storey.

"In the ruins," I said. "The tumbled old cottage."

Old Storey stood up. "Why didn't he come home?"

I looked back at him, not sure what to say. Then Mr. Tuttle's hand settled on my shoulder. "It's Murdoch you should ask," he said.

"Look at him," yelled Storey, coming closer. "How can I do that?"

"Don't shout at the boy," said Mr. Tuttle. "It's no wonder Murdoch was scared to go home."

"Scared?"

"Yes, sir," I said. "He was too frightened to tell you what really happened."

He looked at Murdoch, then at me. "*What* really happened?"

"I can't tell you that," I said.

"You can, boy. And you will." Storey was huge; he towered over Mr. Tuttle.

Mrs. Sims had her veils pulled back, her white face watching. But it was Auntie who spoke. "Stop this nonsense," she cried.

For once it did no good. Old Storey's face was livid with anger, and I closed my eyes, sure he would hit me. But Mr. Tuttle pulled me close against himself and said, "Now, that's enough."

He didn't sound very stern, but he did sound as though he meant it. "I won't have you shouting like this in my house," he said. "Certainly not at Johnny, who did the best he could, and better than most would have done."

Storey was stopped in his tracks. His arms bulged and his eyes showed fury; but he came no closer.

Mr. Tuttle's voice steadied into his schoolteacher's tones. "Now I'll tell you, sir, because I think you should know. Murdoch was shot by his own hand."

Mrs. Sims gasped a shrill breath. Storey staggered back, as though he himself had been shot.

"Johnny kept to his promise and told nobody why," said Mr. Tuttle. "But I imagine your son was afraid that you would see him as something less than a man."

I nodded silently. He had come right to the truth.

The old man went back to the sofa and sat on the table beside it. He took Murdoch's hand, holding it through the blankets. "I want to take him home," he said.

"I won't allow it," said Auntie. "But we'll leave you alone with him, if that's all right with Mr. Tuttle. You can have the house to yourselves if Mr. Tuttle will come and spend Christmas with Johnny and me."

I felt Mr. Tuttle's fingers twitch on my shoulder. "Why, I should like that very much," he said softly.

We left the old man with his soldier son. Mr. Tuttle went pedaling off to send word for the doctor, and caught up with us again just as we reached the gate to Auntie Ivy's house.

CHAPTER 19

December 24, 1914

Dearest Johnny,

I had to write once more before Christmas, and I hope this reaches you in time. I have no more soldiers to send, as I am dashing this off just hours after my last letter. If it's hard to read, or a bit spotted with water, that's because I'm in such an awful hurry. I will be giving this to an officer who is leaving this very moment for his home near Tunbridge Hill, not five miles from where you are. We will be breaking all the rules to do it, but it's the only way I can think of to get this to you in time. There's something I have to tell you.

There won't be an attack, Johnny. There will be no battle on Christmas.

It's an amazing thing, but the Germans are no longer fighting. All along our line—quite suddenly, really—they stopped shooting at us altogether. Right here where I am it's as quiet as a church. The night is just ending and we're seeing a very lovely sunrise—or a little strip of one anyway. It's red and orange, and the brightest yellow that I think I've ever seen. All those colors, in the black frame of our trench, make it look like a stained-glass window. And outside it's so peaceful, so quiet, that I can hardly believe there was ever a war.

Around midnight we heard voices. German voices. They gave us quite a start, as they seemed horribly close, with the air being so quiet and still. But then they started singing, Johnny. They started singing "Silent Night," in lovely deep voices, but all in German of course. So we listened to that carol that we all know so well, and the words didn't make any sense. And it made us feel warm and peaceful and—I don't know what else, it's too hard to say. I think it reminded me, without me really knowing it, about being so young— about being a baby—when I couldn't understand the words even in English. And I felt like a baby must feel, as though nothing can hurt him, as though there's nothing but joy in the world.

The German voices rumbled to us across no-man's-land, and we cried to hear them, Johnny, we really did. We stood sniffing and wiping our eyes, looking up at the stars because that song was just so beautiful. So sad. And when it finished, some of <u>our</u> lads started singing the same carol, with the English words. And the Germans listened to <u>us</u> for a while. Then they joined right in, enemies singing the same song, as perfectly as a church choir. The lads who didn't feel right about singing started to hum along, and they made this melodious drone that swelled and rose across all of no-man's-land, this lovely, quiet hymn.

And then, when we'd finished, one of the Germans called across to us in English. "Good night, Tommies," he said. And someone shouted back, quite gently: "Good night, Fritz."

And Johnny, we wept like schoolgirls.

Now the day is getting bright, and Christmas is very close. And I know there won't be any fighting, you can rest assured of that.

I still wish I were with you, of course. But at least you don't have to worry about me.

Please don't worry about me.

      Love,
      Dad

Mr. Tuttle held his thumbs to his eyes, his hands cupped across his nose. "Good heavens," he said, very softly.

We were sitting at the table, the little tree standing in the middle with all its ornaments shining. Auntie Ivy took off her spectacles and set them down beside it, and they looked like a pair of glass balls that had fallen from the fuzzy branches. Then she folded up the letter.

I thought she would put it with the others, in the wooden box on her bookshelves. But she reached across the table and put it into my hand. "I think you should keep this with you," she said.

"Indeed," added Mr. Tuttle, with a sniff. "You should want to hang on to that."

Auntie pressed the page into my palm, then closed my fingers around it. But I let them spring open again; I let the paper fall away. "It isn't true," I said. I didn't want to hold that letter.

"Whatever do you mean?" said Auntie.

"It's a story," I said.

"A lovely story," said Mr. Tuttle.

"But *not true*." I pushed the letter across the table. It

bounced off the Christmas tree's wooden tub and sat spinning beside it. "Dad *doesn't* sing songs with the Germans."

Poor Mr. Tuttle looked rather stunned. But Auntie Ivy knew what I meant. She said, "How dare you question your father?"

I got up and ran to the door.

As I pulled on my boots, I heard Auntie talking. "He thinks his father is trying to spare him the horrors." I grabbed my coat and went out to the garden.

Christmas Eve was ending. I put my hands to my face and made a slot that I stared through, up at the sky. It was as brown and bleak as the mud; no stained-glass windows for me, only a filthy, splattered pane. I turned as I walked, down from the door, under the tree, and its spidery branches appeared between my hands like spreading cracks on the window of clouds. Then I stumbled, and fell to my knees, looking down at the nutcracker men.

For a whole day I hadn't touched them, yet I was sure they had moved. They stood in a double row, leaning back with their painted faces turned up to watch the sky. For a whole day they hadn't fought, and then Dad's letter had come, in an afternoon post that no one had expected.

"The Germans are no longer fighting."

It seemed impossible, but absolutely true. My wooden soldiers had stopped the war. They had brought a truce, like the one that had come to the Greeks and the Trojans when every man there had prayed for peace.

But then I remembered the billiards table, and the horseshoe pitch that I *knew* didn't exist. And if Dad had invented those, he must have invented the carol.

In Cliffe, the church bells started ringing. They bonged and bonged as I stared down at my nutcracker men, at the others my father had made. Could he really have given them souls?

The bells were ringing the chimes when the door opened and closed behind me. Mr. Tuttle came quietly out to the garden. "The service is starting," he said.

"Do you go to church?" I asked.

"Not very often." He walked past me and crossed, in a step, the no-man's-land between my trenches. In another he was standing behind the British lines, astride my wooden aeroplane. He stooped and picked it up.

"I don't know what to think anymore," I said.

"About what?" he asked.

"Anything." The bells rang through their chorus, both discordant and lovely. "I was so excited at first. With the war."

"We all were," said Mr. Tuttle.

"But I hate it already. And it's just going to go on and on."

Mr. Tuttle flicked the little propeller. It made a humming sound.

"And what if it's one of those that last a hundred years?"

"I doubt that's the case, Johnny," he said. "We're getting better at fighting wars. We've got them running like machines now: faster, more efficient."

"I wish we'd get better at *not* fighting them," I said.

"That's a fine thought," said Mr. Tuttle.

The bells stopped ringing, their last tingles of sound seeming to linger on. "I think Auntie would like to go to church," I said.

"Would she?"

I nodded. "We haven't been there before."

"I'll show you the way," said Mr. Tuttle.

He carried the aeroplane into the house, and in the doorway he started to fly it. His arm zoomed up and down; his doughy lips made engine noises, a bomb whistling down and bursting. Then he blushed and gave me the toy. I set it on the table, beside the little Christmas tree.

We walked to the church, and Storey Sims's black horse was still harnessed to its wagon. Mr. Tuttle said it was the strangest thing he'd ever done to pass his house and see light inside. "I'd rather thought it was a lonely house, but it looks quite cheery," he said. Auntie Ivy said she'd always liked it, that she'd wished sometimes that she lived there. Then she laughed, embarrassed, and the sound of it tingled in the air like the last of the bells.

The church was ancient and cold. We found room in the first pew, and Mr. Tuttle—in a whisper—told me I was sitting where Normans had sat, where knights and their ladies had sat, where Dickens himself might have sat. We stood and sang carols, then knelt and prayed for the soldiers.

"We ask God to keep them safe," said the minister. "We ask that He lay His hand on their heads, each and every one, and bestow upon them His ever-loving mercy."

My eyes were closed. I saw that huge white hand forming in the clouds, running first down the British line, and then down the Germans'. He would bless them all, I thought; they were all the same to Him.

Then we got to our feet, in a great stamping and a

rumble of coughs. And I sang "Silent Night" with Auntie Ivy piping away on my left and Mr. Tuttle humming on my other side. And I looked up at the altar, higher to the stained-glass windows that someone had made when England was young. They were dark shapes, just holes in the stones. But as we sang they started to glow, the moon coming out for a moment. And red light, and yellow, fell through the church, and I felt as though nothing could hurt me. I felt as a baby must feel.

The moon was hidden when we left for home, as though it hadn't come out at all. Cliffe seemed small and pretty, like a toy village come to life. As we walked through it the rain started, gently but chill as ice. The night was so cold that Auntie Ivy had to reach across me and put her hand into Mr. Tuttle's pocket just to keep it warm.

I didn't go in when they did. I said I had to see to my soldiers, and though Auntie Ivy said she wished I didn't, Mr. Tuttle said a little while wouldn't hurt, and he'd come out and fetch me when tea was made. So I crouched by myself in the garden as Christmas Eve ended, and I brought all the nutcracker men out of their trenches. I brought all the British out of theirs, all the Frenchmen too. And I stood them together in no-man's-land, though one was missing because I couldn't find General Cedric.

When Mr. Tuttle came out, I had them in a big bunch with the old broken model of my father right in the middle. The sleeping soldier, who couldn't stand up by himself, leaned on a nutcracker man. And the nutcracker men mingled in with the Frenchmen. And Fatty Dienst stood next to Dad, beside a messman with his pots.

"What are they doing?" asked Mr. Tuttle.

"They're praying for peace," I said. "Like the Trojans and the Greeks."

He nodded, his hands in his pockets. "Is that what you're hoping for?"

"Oh, I don't know if it matters," I said. "They might only be wooden men."

"With their own little truce in the garden, you mean?"

"Yes, sir," I said.

"That's good enough," he told me.

Then we went inside, and I smelled the pudding boiling. I heard the chatter of its lid as it boiled in the pot, cooking for Christmas dinner. And I saw that the tree had been moved, from the table to a stool, and there was a small pile of presents below it.

"Are those for me?" I asked.

"Yes," said Auntie Ivy. "Your mother sent them some time ago. There's a card to go with them."

"Can you read it now?" I asked.

"Certainly not," she said. "Only heathens open gifts on Christmas Eve."

CHAPTER 20

December 24, 1914

My dear little Johnny,

I must be the luckiest woman in the world to have you for a son. All the women here at Woolwich are forever talking about their children and what little horrors they are. I tell them about you, and they say that mine must be an angel. They're right, you know.

But it's funny, Johnny. I'm so lucky but oh soooo miserable. I didn't think I would ever, ever, EVER spend a Christmas without you.

The work at the arsenal never stops. But I'm helping the war, and we all have to make our sacrifices. I know how brave you are, and I'm sure you'll understand.

Well, I hope you're having a merry Christmas in Kent. I hope you have sunshine and snow, and a chance to go sleighing. Most of all, I hope that we're all together again next year.

I miss you and your father very, very much.
Love,
Mum

"Well, she's almost right," said Auntie Ivy, passing the card to me. "At least we have sunshine."

"And it's sort of snowy," I said.

The ground had frozen, and the frost was thick and white. It glowed so bright in the morning sun that I had to squint to see it. And a layer of ice covered the trees, turning every branch into clusters of diamonds, each little twig into a sparkling, feathery frond.

I looked at the card, at its picture of a huge old sleigh pulled by horses with ribbons and bells. Then I opened the presents that Mum had sent: red mittens dangling tassels; a mechanical bear that rode on a bicycle; the *Boys Own Annual*.

I opened them all in a hurry, kneeling on the floor as Mr. Tuttle and Auntie watched from their chairs. Then I thought of Mum with her hands going yellow, picking the presents out from a shop, wrapping them up to send me. I thought of Dad in his trench, with no-man's-land a big frosty field, with the sun on his face, and his beard all icy. And I started to cry because they were so far away.

"Well, that's a *fine* thing," snapped Auntie. "Crying on Christmas Day. What a shameful thing to do."

But Mr. Tuttle understood. "Now, Ivy," he said, gently. "You must not have been a child who was sent away for Christmas." He was all rumply from sleeping in his armchair, and he smoothed his wrinkled sleeves. "I remember very well my first Christmas in a boarding school. In all my years, I've never felt so miserable as that."

"Oh dear," said Auntie Ivy. "I'm sorry, Hubert."

I giggled; I'd never heard his proper name before.

"Enough of that," he said, pretending to be stern.

And then to Auntie Ivy, "I think Johnny should be sent to the pantry."

"Yes, I think he should too," said Auntie.

They were smiling at each other, their heads tilted, like a pair of pigeons. "Off you go, then," said Mr. Tuttle.

"Why?" I asked.

"Oh, one never knows," he said, as though Christmas had made him giddy.

I wound up my bear and sent him rattling across the floor. Then I got up and went to the pantry. And there was a bicycle standing inside.

It was red and silver, with a basket on the front. I wheeled it out, knowing better than to ride it through the house.

"That's from Mr. Tuttle and I," said Auntie.

"Tuttle and *me*," the old schoolteacher said.

I was grinning. "It's super!" I cried.

Auntie Ivy stood up and hugged me. "Now go outside and amuse yourself for a while. We're all going to walk to Mr. Tuttle's and see how Murdoch is faring."

"Can I take my bicycle out?" I asked.

"Absolutely not," she said. "You'd break your neck before you passed the gate."

Mr. Tuttle walked with me to the door. He put his hand on my back. "Merry Christmas, Johnny," he said.

"Thank you, sir," I told him.

I thought he wanted to hug me but was too shy to do it. His hand ran up my back as I stooped to get my boots. It rubbed on my head; then his fingertips scraped through my hair, as though he held on as long as he could.

"This isn't likely the last wartime Christmas," he said. "You might be here for quite a long time, Johnny."

"I've thought of that," I said.

"You won't see your father for a while. And I'm sorry for you, I really am. But while you're here; only while you're here—" He coughed. "Well, you see, I think I'll be staying in Cliffe. And a boy should have someone he can go to with his troubles."

"I already do," I said.

He looked at me and slowly smiled. "Oh, Johnny, thank you," he said.

I wished he wasn't so shy. But I could see that he wasn't going to hug me, so I flapped my hands and said, "I'd better go out." And he opened the door, with a huge grin on his face.

The frost crunched under my boots. The sun glared on the ice, on the trees and the wall, and the fields of Kent looked like carpets of jewels. Even the wooden soldiers were covered with frost, all of them sparkling below me.

On the porch was the box that my mother had sent, its top torn open. I dragged it down, across the garden, under the tree with its diamond branches. And I started packing away my Tommies and my nutcracker men.

They had frozen together, as though the British soldiers were embracing the Germans, as though they'd huddled for warmth in the cold. In France, the battle might have started; it might have finished then. But I didn't think I would ever play at war again.

The soldiers bounced into the empty box, then knocked against each other. I put them all together, Fatty Dienst and all my Germans, the dog-faced man and the messman and the drum and trumpet players. I found General Cedric, looking cold and alone, and put him in as well. But my little broken dad I kept aside; I thought I'd stand him by my bed, and just wait for the day he came home.

I dragged the box back to the house, and no one asked me why. Mr. Tuttle was putting on his old gray overcoat. He had only one arm in its sleeve, and with his other he was helping Auntie Ivy, holding her crimson jacket. I left my box in the hall, and together we all set off for Mr. Tuttle's house.

It was almost noon when we got there. The sky was clouding over, but the weather stayed bitterly cold. Storey Sims's black horse was the only thing in all the world not covered with frost. It stood, with ice at its nostrils, like a great lump of coal in the middle of a whitewashed floor. The wagon glittered with ice: its wheels were like frozen Catherine wheels; even the reins sparkled with frost.

We didn't go in the front, but around the back with Mr. Tuttle leading. I didn't understand why until I thought of his roses, and how he must have fretted about them all night and all day. He went straight to their corner, and when he touched them the ice shivered away from their branches.

I heard a sound of engines, and looked up to the north. Above the marshes, an aeroplane was flying west toward London. The sun glinted on its wings as it banked and straightened.

I knew the shape of those wings, the curve of the tail. "An FF twenty-nine," I said. "A German."

"Really?" said Auntie Ivy.

Mr. Tuttle turned away from his roses. We watched

the aeroplane, and saw two others behind it, black specks coming from the east, from Grain. The German turned slightly north.

"He's going to bomb London," I said.

The planes were so small, London so distant, that I felt only excited at the idea of it. I thought of the soldiers at their gun and how they would jump to their feet, spilling the tea from their metal cups.

The engines buzzed, barely louder than flies. The German rolled sideways, and straightened, and the other machines came into line behind it.

"A Vickers," I said. "And the Albatros, look!" It seemed funny that a machine built in Germany would be sent up to knock a German down. And I doubted that it could. "The German's faster," I said. "They might not catch him."

They flitted past a line of trees, the German, then the British. And when they appeared again, the aeroplanes were closer together.

"No, I don't believe he's going all the way to London," said Mr. Tuttle. "He'll be after the arsenal at Woolwich."

My excitement vanished, and a sickly fear took its place.

"The arsenal's packed with powder," said Mr. Tuttle. If he ever knew my mum was there he had forgotten it now. "We'll feel the blast from here."

"My mother's in Woolwich!" I cried.

"Oh," he said, in a tiny voice. His eyes were wide, and his mouth stayed open in a little circle.

The FF29 went down in a dive. It dropped below the hedges around us, and we could only hear the sound of its motor speeding into a whine. The British pilots dipped and followed it.

"This can't be real," said Auntie Ivy. "It can't be true."

A gun opened up somewhere by the river. Little black clouds dotted across the sky, along the top of the hedge beside us. And it was the worst feeling in the world to know there was nothing we could do.

Then the sounds of the engines changed again. They grew clearer, and louder, and the German machine appeared suddenly, far in the west. It came toward us, maybe a thousand feet up, growing larger, tilting left and then right in slashes of sunshine. The British were above it, still behind it, and another Vickers had appeared.

The German machine had clumsy floats instead of wheels. It carried a pair of bombs slung on a rack between them. It came roaring straight at us.

"Get to the house!" shouted Mr. Tuttle. "Go on." He shoved Auntie Ivy, and she skidded on the frost. He pushed again; she fell to her knees. "Johnny, help her!"

I ran to take her elbow, thinking that Mr. Tuttle would take the other. But he only pressed us together, gave us another push forward, then turned away himself.

He crossed the garden in his clumsy run, shattering the frost with his shoes. His coat flapped around him, tangling at his legs, and he thrashed at it as he stumbled along.

I looked up at the FF29. It skittered on the air like a boat on the sea, flung up and tossed down, tipped to its right, then its left. But it still came toward us.

"Hubert!" shouted Auntie Ivy. She was looking back at Mr. Tuttle.

I couldn't believe what he was doing. In the corner of the garden he wrestled with his big pile of boards.

"Hubert!"

He didn't look up. "My roses," he said. "I have to shield Glory."

"Oh, please," she wailed.

He pulled at the boards, but the frost stuck them together. He kicked at the pile, and a white shower of sparkles rose from his foot. And the German tilted down in a dive.

Its wings stretched as wide as the house. Its propeller spun in a blur. And it swooped from the sky, no longer a machine flown by a man, but a thing with eyes, with a mind.

"Hubert, please!"

The door to the house flew open, and old Storey Sims came lumbering out. "Are you mad?" he shouted. "Don't you see that machine?"

"Help my auntie," I said.

He dashed to her side and plucked her clear from the ground. He carried her as though she weighed nothing at all. And I ran to help Mr. Tuttle.

"Get inside," he said.

"No, sir," I told him.

He had a board lifted half from the pile. I got my shoulder underneath and levered it up, and it sprang loose from the others with a loud rip, like a scream. We heaved it up, one end on the wall, and there it lay, slanted in front of the roses, a tiny shield just six inches wide.

"Another," I said.

Mr. Tuttle was panting. "No time," he said.

The German was crossing the field beyond the road, rushing on at a hundred miles an hour. I heard the black horse whinny with fright; I heard its harness jangle.

"Get down!" shouted Mr. Tuttle.

He dropped to his belly, onto the frost. His hand groped out to find me, to pull me down. But I stepped away and went back to the wood. I had destroyed his roses, and I would do what I could to save them.

The board wouldn't lift, and the seaplane hurtled over the road. I saw the pilot, helmeted and goggled. I saw the British coming after him. And we stared at each other, through the blurred propeller, as I clawed at the wood with my fingers.

I saw him move, and I thought now the bombs would fall. I watched to see them drop.

It might have been that the pilot never meant to drop his bombs. He might only have been weaving away from the Vickers. Possibly, he saw a better target to the south. But the thought that came to me was that he just couldn't drop a bomb on a child, that he couldn't kill a boy on Christmas Day. And the pilot snapped his machine onto its side, and the tail flaps hinged as he banked away to the south.

He flew over my head with a deafening clatter, and the Vickers, then the Albatros, passed behind him.

Mr. Tuttle looked up. There was a bead of frost on the tip of his nose. "You could have been killed, Johnny. What were you thinking?"

"I had to help you," I said. "I was the one who damaged your roses."

"You?"

"Yes, sir."

"Why?"

"For my Guy Fawkes guy."

"My beautiful roses?" he said.

"I'm sorry, sir," I said.

"Why couldn't you tell me?" asked Mr. Tuttle.

"I was scared to at first," I said. "And then I was ashamed."

"Even after this morning?" He looked puzzled more than sad. "Even after our talk you couldn't come to me with this?"

"No, sir," I said.

"But why on earth not?"

We heard the bombs explode then. Two geysers of mud appeared in the south, toward the railway tracks and the station. They grew higher, roiling with dust and smoke, and the British machines went tearing through them in pursuit of the vanishing German. Then the mud fell down in a rain.

Between us and the raining mud a flock of rooks went whirling up, like bits of shrapnel flung about. And the air sort of crumpled around us, and we heard the bangs, and they scared me badly. The windows rattled in Mr. Tuttle's house, and the blast echoed like far-off thunder. The aeroplanes flew off to the east, the German weaving ahead of the British.

The sound brought Storey Sims out from the house. It brought Auntie Ivy and Murdoch, too. The young soldier leaned on his father. He looked ill and ridden with pain, but I could see he would live after all. The three of them stared up at the sky, warily, as though the bombs had fallen from nowhere, and another could follow at any moment.

Then Murdoch asked me, "Do you see what I meant?"

"Yes," I said. It would drive me mad to hear bombs burst all around me, all day and all night, to feel the air thicken and warp, and to wonder if someone I knew had been blown into smithereens.

"Thank you for bringing me home," said Murdoch.

Old Storey held his son, and Mr. Tuttle looked at them, and then at me. He cocked his head in a quizzical way. "Ahh," he said. Then he came to my side, and his coat—flapping out—wrapped around me. I knew that he understood why I hadn't told him about the roses; and I knew that I *could,* whenever I wanted, tell him my darkest secrets with no fear that he would think any less of me.

We went up to the door. He hugged Auntie Ivy, and she ran her hands all over his back, as though to make sure the bomb hadn't knocked him to pieces. And then we all went inside, as the church bells rang for Christmas Day.

Chapter 21

December 26, 1914

My dearest Johnny,
I woke in the trenches on Christmas morning and could
hardly believe my eyes. The sun was just rising, and it shone
across a land so white that I was sure all of Flanders was
covered with snow. But you probably saw that too, as you're
really so very close to where I am.
I heard shouting from the men at the parapets. The Huns
were moving, they said. The Huns were coming.
I leapt up, my rifle ready. I laid it down on the sandbags
and squinted through the sights. And right before me, just
thirty yards away, there was a line of shapes that was dark
against the sun. But they sparkled, those shapes. I couldn't
make them out until the sun rose a little higher. And then I
saw they were Christmas trees, and they were decorated with
tinsel and garlands.
A German voice shouted out, "Tommies, don't shoot!"
And a man came up from the trench, between the trees. He
walked toward us across that frosty no-man's-land, slowly
and calmly, like a fellow out for a stroll in the park. Then

one of our lieutenants scrambled up, and he started across to meet him.

At the wire, they shook hands. They each stepped back a pace, and they saluted one another. And I tell you, it was the most amazing thing to see them standing all alone in that land of white, where no two men had ever stood, and likely will never stand again. The Christmas trees sparkled with their garlands and tinsel; the frost glittered with incredible brilliance.

And then the Germans came out from their trench, and we came out from ours. All of us spilled up onto that awful, beautiful ground.

We drank German beer and ate British chocolate. We took snaps of each other, the Germans in their gray, the British in our motley clothes of fur and wool, all standing arm in arm between the trenches. Everyone got out their wallets and showed each other pictures. Someone found a football, and a little game broke out.

Remember the doorman from around the corner? Willy Kempf's his name. Well, he was there, and we talked about London and he asked about you. I tried to find Fatty Dienst but, sadly, he wasn't there. Just a few days earlier I would have met him, but by Christmas he was—Well, Johnny, he was gone.

All day we went back and forth, from the Germans' trench to ours. I gave a man the packet of matches that Princess Mary sent me. And in exchange he gave me a razor; a very fine razor, in fact. I thought I would hang on to it until you're old enough to shave, but I decided that I would send it now, as it's such a splendid keepsake from the most amazing Christmas I have ever seen.

You'll find it, enclosed.

Toward nightfall, the Germans lit the candles on their trees. Hundreds of little flames twinkled away, shining in the frost like so many stars. We sang "Silent Night" again, and "O Tannenbaum."

Then the generals got wind of our truce. They were furious that we were talking to Fritz instead of trying to shoot him. They chased us to our trench, and the Germans' generals chased them to theirs. If it wasn't for the generals we might never have gone back to the war.

In the morning, two Germans stood up on their parapet. They opened a long banner that they'd made out of blankets. They'd painted across it: "Merry Christmas, Tommies." They saluted us, and one of them pulled out a pistol and fired twice in the air. Then they carefully wound up their banner and dropped back in the trench.

And a little while later the shooting started, and the war was on again.

Merry Christmas, Johnny.

> *All my love,*
> *Dad*

The letter came three days after Christmas, and by then I already knew what had happened. Dad was telling the truth, word for word, just as it happened. There had been no billiards, no horseshoes, but that truce on Christmas Day was very, very real.

The trenches stretched from the Channel to Switzerland. Across all of Europe, over hills and down into valleys, through forests and fields, over rivers and streams, the Germans and the British had fought just yards apart. But here and there, on Christmas Day, the war stopped for a while, and the enemies became friends. British soldiers and German soldiers met in no-man's-land. They exchanged presents and photographs. In one or two places they even played football.

I would never see anything as close to a miracle as that Christmas of 1914. Maybe the peace would have spread along the whole front, across the whole world, if it hadn't been for the generals. They chased their men back to the trenches; they ordered them to start shooting again. But for a day, at least, the war stopped; it happened that once and never again.

I don't know if my wooden soldiers had anything to do with the Christmas truce. I really didn't want to know. The box where I'd put them on Christmas morning stayed under my bed for nearly four years, until my dad came home at last.

My mum was wearing long white gloves when she met him at the station. Underneath, her hands were yellow, stained by the sulphur from her shells. For the next five years she wore the gloves nearly night and day, and the ghastly color never left her. Though my dad escaped the war, my mum did not. She died in 1923, still young and beautiful.

Mr. Tuttle became my Uncle Hubert. He married Auntie in the big stone church where we'd gone on Christmas Eve. His best man was Murdoch, who stood beside him on crutches, because he had lost his leg to gangrene.

I got used to seeing the sergeant that way. Always cheery, always laughing, he hopped along like a three-legged bird, never tiring on the walks we took together. The orange cat became his pet and sometimes followed us as far as the gate, but never beyond it. Murdoch took a new name, and all of Cliffe kept his secret. Even Auntie Ivy never breathed a word about Murdoch's self-inflicted wound. He started writing poems; he had them published, too. Most were about Kent, about the fields and the sun and the rainbows. But sometimes he would go into a gloom and write about the war. And what he wrote then made people cry.

When Dad came home, looking thinner and older, I gave Murdoch my box of wooden soldiers. He was looking after his own father then, and it wouldn't be long until old Storey was laid down in the little cemetery with all the other Simses. I carried the box to his farmhouse, and Storey and Murdoch both helped me unpack it.

We stood the soldiers in rows on a bookshelf. And there they still stand, as far as I know. Or some of them, anyway.

Murdoch wrote a poem about them when he was quite an old man. He said how they made him think of the friends he'd made in the army, how the nutcracker men were aging like them, gathering dust on their wooden shoulders. Every once in a while, he said, often in the dead of night, one of those fierce-looking men would suddenly tip over. It would roll from the shelf and land on the floor with a little thunk. He said that by then there weren't many left.

AUTHOR'S NOTE

They called it the Great War.

It started in August 1914 and ended on November 11, 1918. Sixty million soldiers and sailors and airmen took part, representing sixteen nations. Of every three men sent to fight, one was wounded; of every eight, one was killed.

My mother's three uncles went off with Lovat's Scouts, in the Highland Regiment. All three were taken prisoner. My father's father lied about his age to join the British Army when he was seventeen. He went to France with the Cambridshires, a battalion of the Suffolk Regiment. While serving in the trenches as a Lewis gunner, he was wounded by shrapnel. But he went back to the fighting and lost an arm. In May 1917 he was sent home to England. For the rest of his life he wore a contraption of leather and metal to take the place of his missing hand. He was troubled until the day that he died by the shrapnel that remained inside him.

I never met any of them. But as a child I saw other veterans of the Great War. Some had no legs. They sat on little wooden platforms fitted with wheels. They pushed themselves along the sidewalks and sold pencils on street corners. I remember my mother pulling me past one. "Don't stare," she told me. "Don't stare."

When I was older I read about the war, about Billy Bishop and the Red Baron, Lawrence of Arabia and Count Luckner the Sea Devil. I never connected them with the old men on the streets. They were preserved in my books, forever young. The war that killed millions, and crippled millions more, produced a few heroes. And it produced a few miracles, too.

The Christmas Truce of 1914 really did happen. Along whole sections of the Western Front, the fighting stopped for that first Christmas of the war. Soldiers came out of the trenches to meet in no-man's-land, exchanging presents and pictures. Just hours before, they had shot at each other. Now they shook hands and sang carols.

The Angel of Mons was true as well, or at least there were many who claimed to have seen that vision in the sky. It was only the first of many such stories. There was something about the Great War that inspired a belief in the supernatural. There were ghostly soldiers and phantom cavalry, and an airman who simply vanished. There were soldiers convinced that the ghosts of English archers appeared in the night to hold the same bit of ground against the Germans that they'd held against the French five hundred years before. In the morning, the story goes, German soldiers covered the ground, their bodies riddled with arrows.

Cliffe is real. It's a charming little village beside the marshes of the Thames. On Christmas Day in 1914, a

German airman really did drop a bomb near Cliffe's railway station. The raid wasn't quite as dramatic as Johnny tells it, as the aeroplanes didn't come so close to the ground. But visitors are still taken to see the place where the bomb came down.

There were men like Johnny's father who volunteered in October and were in the field by Christmas. But there weren't very many. In the first feverish weeks of the war, most of the volunteers joined the "new army" being raised by Lord Kitchener, a hero of the Boer War and—in 1914—Britain's secretary of state for war. While the generals thought the war would end quickly, Kitchener believed it would last three years and planned his recruitment for that. His thousands of volunteers spent months parading through streets and parks, while the "old army," desperate for men, sent its few new recruits into battle as quickly as possible.

When Johnny's father arrived in France, the war was settling into its stalemate. The armies were only then beginning to build the elaborate trenches that would be their homes for four years. The strip of Europe that would be reduced to a wasteland was still dotted with farms and trees. But sectors of the front were just as described by Johnny's father. I have tried not to be influenced by the horrors that were yet to come, by the poison gas and flamethrowers and corpse-choked ground that were all unimagined in 1914.

Through it all, the mail went back and forth. The letters from Johnny's father may seem to come with unlikely regularity and impossible speed, but the truth is that they don't. Mail from the front was delivered in

England within two or three days. The battlefield, for many British soldiers, was so close to home that it was heartbreaking.

An officer going on leave could have breakfast in the trenches and supper in a London hotel. The soldier at the front could read a newspaper just one day old. During the biggest barrages, the sound of guns was heard in England.

I imagine that my grandfather could hear them for the rest of his life.

ACKNOWLEDGMENTS

This book started as a Christmas story, as a simple tale of a boy and his wooden soldiers. It grew into what it is through the help of many people.

Bruce Wishart introduced me to nutcracker men. He shaped the figures, then helped shape the story through many conversations.

My parents provided answers to many questions about day-to-day life in Britain. When they didn't have the answer, my father found it. He provided books and research material, then corrected many mistakes that I'd made.

As with every book I've written, I owe thanks to my companion, Kristin Miller, and my agent, Jane Jordan Browne, and to the people at Random House, especially Françoise Bui. All of them provided much support and encouragement, as they always do.

But this story could not have been written without the help of Kathleen Larkin, a research librarian at the Prince Rupert Library. She spent countless hours immersed in the Great War, finding just the right book to answer the most obscure question, or the particular person who knew what even the books didn't tell. She even went to Cliffe and sent me pictures of a village that was far more lovely and picturesque than the one I'd imagined for myself.

These are just some of the people who answered her queries, who helped me portray a period that is, sadly, being quickly forgotten:

Mrs. Peggy Wise and Mr. David Wright, proprietors of Martins News in Cliffe, Kent.

Pat Leviston of Cliffe, Kent.

Michele Losse, research assistant at Post Office Heritage Services in London.

Major Vince Larocque, museum curator for the Canadian Military Engineers, in Vancouver.

Marion Webster of the Guildhall Museum in Rochester, Kent.

Angela Woollacott, professor, historian, and author, of Case Western Reserve University in Cleveland.

Miss Eileen N. Hawkins, of the YWCA in London.

John A. Henshall, librarian, at the University of Warwick library in Coventry.

Barbara Ludlow of Hawkinge, Kent.

The staff of the Imperial War Museum, London.

Derek Reid of British Telecom Archives, London.

Sergeant Pilkington of the Philatelic Bureau of the British Forces Post Office in London.

Liliane Reid Lafleur and Ray White of the library of the Canadian War Museum in Ottawa.

Penny McLaughlin, commemoration and public relations, Veterans Affairs Canada.

Jim Streckfuss, president of the League of World War I Aviation Historians.

ABOUT THE AUTHOR

Iain Lawrence studied journalism in Vancouver, British Columbia, and worked for small newspapers in the northern part of the province. He settled on the coast, living first in the port city of Prince Rupert and now on the Gulf Islands. An avid sailor, he wrote two nonfiction books about his travels on the coast before turning to children's novels. *Lord of the Nutcracker Men* was inspired, in part, by family stories of his grandfather, who served as a Lewis gunner on the Western Front during World War I.

Lawrence is the author of four other novels for young readers, including the acclaimed High Seas Trilogy: *The Wreckers* (an Edgar Allan Poe Award Nominee), *The Smugglers,* and *The Buccaneers. Ghost Boy,* set in postwar America, was named a *Publishers Weekly* Best Book of the Year, a *School Library Journal* Best Book of the Year, an ALA Best Book for Young Adults, and an ALA Notable Book.